SON OF MAN

The Gospel According to Beverli

by
Beverli Jinn

PublishAmerica
Baltimore

First printing

This is a work of fiction set in a background of history. Public personages both living and dead may appear in the story under their right names. Scenes and dialogue involving them with fictitious characters are of course invented. Any other usage of real people's names is coincidental. Any resemblance of the imaginary characters to actual persons, living or dead, is entirely coincidental.

At the specific preference of the author, PublishAmerica allowed this work to remain exactly as the author intended, verbatim, without editorial input.

ISBN: 1-4241-5569-X
PUBLISHED BY PUBLISHAMERICA, LLLP
www.publishamerica.com
Baltimore

Printed in the United States of America

Author's Note

The term 'Son of Man' is often used in a titular sense, suggesting that the person referred to is an apocalyptic figure, the designated agent for God's judgment on an evil world. The canonical gospels clearly use the term to refer to Jesus in this way.

According to John Dominic Crossan, however, in his book *Jesus: A Revolutionary Biography*, Jesus did not consider himself an apocalyptic figure. "Jesus," Crossan claims, "used the generic term 'son of man' to identify himself with those he was addressing, to emphasize that he shared with them a common destiny as *we* poor or destitute human beings."

Son of Man is a story about Jesus' humanity, not his divinity.

Foreword

Son of Man is a work of fiction or, perhaps, creative nonfiction. What else can it be? After all, very little is known of the life of Jesus of Nazareth. Was Joseph his father? Did Jesus have siblings? Where was he born? How and where was he educated? Was he ever a carpenter? Was he ever married? Did he have children? What did he do for thirty years before Mark picked up his story at the River Jordan?

And those are the easy questions!

Just who were the writers of the New Testament gospels? Few modern scholars believe that the writers of these gospels, men (?) who wrote under the names of Mark, Mathew, Luke, and John, were contemporaries of Jesus. These gospel authors never heard Jesus speak. They never witnessed Jesus' healing. They never sat with him or walked with him or taught with him.

The source of their knowledge about Jesus? Oral tradition—stories passed along from person to person for half a century or longer—tales borrowed from humankind's eternal storytelling passion, tales ill-remembered, tales embellished within the framework of the teller's own experience and imagination.

Oh, yes, there are those who believe that God himself inspired these gospel writers, enabling them to get the story right. And why not? Certainly the Creator of the Universe should be capable of getting the Word out with accuracy and precision. Why not believe that these gospels represent the inerrant Word of God? Wouldn't the Creator want humankind to understand? What would be the point in creating creatures that had no clue about why they exist? And what was the easiest way to make them understand? Tell them! Or, at least, tell a few of them and instruct those few to tell everyone else.

This line of reasoning asks us to believe that, even though self-aware creatures had existed for perhaps two million years, the One God didn't get around to clarifying his relationship with them until about 1,300 B.C.E. when he met with Moses on a mountain and laid down the Law, the most important precept being, "You shall have no other gods before Me." Up until that time, human beings had invented their own gods, as many as they wanted—or not.

Of course, humankind couldn't be satisfied with just one prophet's report. While the Jewish people found it necessary to modify Moses' God only minimally, Buddhism, Hinduism, Shintoism, Christianity, Islam, and a whole raft of other religious systems sprang up, each with its own subdivisions that further polarized people as they strove to answer the Great Question: "What's it all about?" There certainly has been no shortage of Great Prophets who have claimed to have the answers. And each of these Great Prophets has been embraced by lesser holy men who have taken it upon themselves to interpret and disseminate their version of Cosmic Truth.

The really distressing thing about this entire process is that these confidants of the One God don't agree on the nature of the Creator or the message of the Creator. If God speaks to selected human beings and guides their hand as they record his Word, wouldn't you think that he would give the same message to each?

Must we conclude that most of the prophets don't have it right? This is the easiest road to take. It then remains only to decide which message is the correct one. Once the choice is made, the others can be discounted.

An alternative, albeit a frustrating one, is to conclude that *all* of the great teachers are correct, that the Creator is so complex that human beings are incapable of understanding the whole. We can attain brief glimpses of the Great Mystery but can never understand its depth or express its wonder with any degree of satisfaction.

And so, while the synoptic gospels and the Gospel of John often disagree with one another, this need not be a problem. Most scholars agree that Mark's gospel was written first, probably about 70 C.E., his work relying a lot on a source called Q, which no longer exists. Mathew was next and then Luke, each of these writers borrowing heavily from Mark but each adding or eliminating events and sayings, each presenting a point of view all his own.

Toward the end of the first century, John wrote his gospel, including some of what had appeared in the synoptic gospels but presenting a Jesus who was not a storyteller but a person fond of lofty language and lengthy oratory. At the Last Supper, the Jesus of Mark, Mathew, and Luke speaks briefly about the bread and wine that represents his body and his blood. In John's gospel, however, after washing the disciples' feet, Jesus delivers a six page oration announcing his departure, stating that he is the way, the truth, and the life, promising the arrival of another helper, the Holy Spirit, proclaiming himself "the true vine", and concluding with a lengthy prayer for himself and for his disciples. There is no mention of bread or wine.

Who, then, has it right? Did all of these things happen, or none of them? Did Jesus use parables to make his point, or did he make long speeches? Did he overturn the tables of the moneychangers early in his ministry or just before his death? Did he deliver a Sermon on the Mount? Did his ministry last three years or just one?

The answer is that Mark told his Truth, Mathew his, Luke his, and John his. They were not reporting objectively. They were not reporting documented facts. They were writing very personal, very subjective accounts of the life of the Messiah they wanted Jesus to be. And they were not alone. Dozens of other writers wrote dozens of other gospels, each reporting his own Truth. Were they all writing the inspired Word of God? Absolutely—canonized by the Church or not!

And, contrary to what seems to be a general misunderstanding, God has not stopped talking to humankind. Throughout the past 2,006 years, God has been talking and prophets have been listening and reporting. The job description for the position of prophet does not include predicting the future. It requires only that the prophet do his best to listen and to share the message that he hears. Every human being is potentially the right man for the job.

It's all part of a bazillion piece jigsaw puzzle that will not make complete sense until every piece is in place. In the meantime, what fun to search and question! What fun to envision the whole! What fun to live in the kingdom of heaven!

The Prophetess Beverli

1

Somehow more vulnerable stripped of his clothing, he shivers uncontrollably. It is only partly that he is cold. The spring day is warm enough. It is that he is afraid—terribly afraid. He wills himself to rise above the fear, to reject the impending pain, to accept with equanimity the imminent horror of the iron-fingered whip.

His mind only vaguely acknowledges the soldiers as they tie his hands to a post. Shutting down. Shutting down. At last, escaping the Nowness that had imprisoned his being, he slips into a warm, lightless peace, nourished within the womb of his Soul.

To his right—always to his right—the Jordan wound snakelike along its eternal journey through the barren height that was the wilderness, curving and twisting in every direction, sometimes flowing in musical silence past a low shore of tamarisk, willow, and thick, high cane, sometimes rushing wildly between high, rocky banks.

Nine days earlier he'd left Nazareth, heading east to the Sea of Galilee before directing his steps southward, in no hurry yet eager to reach the area near the Dead Sea where the man called John the Baptist was attracting crowds—something about repentance, something about the long awaited messiah, something about the destruction of mankind.

It was an easy, well-traveled route despite the irregular terrain and the dust that covered his feet and clung to his clothing and sucked the moisture from his skin, despite the burning sun that made it impossible to make progress except during the hours of early morning and late evening. The cool pure water of the river was a constant. Never was there a problem clambering down its sandy bluffs and reaching the shade and serenity of the tree-lined, reedy banks. Never was there a sense of urgency. If he chose to linger and admire a hawk perched on the top of a blighted tree or to enjoy the chirruping of a bulbul from the overhanging boughs, he was free to do so. If he chose to engage in conversation, idle or provocative, with a fellow traveler, he joyfully engaged. There was much to discuss, much to learn, much to share.

On the morning of the tenth day he was able to discern in the distance the spread of green that he was looking for, an oasis of tamarisk and palm trees, reeds and grasses that spread perhaps two miles east of the Jordan where it emptied into the Dead Sea. If the stories were correct, it was here that he would find John the Baptist, and now, as the spring-fed wadi took shape before him, he caught himself hurrying his step. A strange sense of purpose began to churn inside him, an inexplicable sense that he'd recognized weeks, months—maybe even years—earlier, a nagging, indefinable restlessness that only now was shaping itself into something more, still indefinable but no longer to be put aside.

The sun had crossed overhead by the time he reached the wadi at its northeastern limits, behind him the barren wilderness, ahead of him a thick belt of trees and bushes that stretched for some distance westward to the river, and to his left an elevated slope pockmarked with caves. The area before him promised a cool, gurgling coolness, and from this high ground at the edge it was easy to imagine quiet pathways and a shady serenity cooled by spring-fed pools and streams that found their way downward to the marshlands of the Jordan. From somewhere—nowhere—an occasional voice broke the stillness, more an unobtrusive reminder of human presence than an identifiable word or phrase. Sometimes it was a distant shout, but mostly it was a vague murmur of life that seemed an integral part of the peace rather than an intrusion.

He slid down a soft, chalky bank and was soon working his way along the nearest path, enjoying a significant drop in temperature as he left the shimmering heat of the desert and entered the shady humidity of spring-fed rivulets oozing from the muddy earth and collecting in rocky pools. Inevitably, he knew, there would be larger pools as he moved away from the caves behind him and toward the Jordan in the distance, but he came upon the first one sooner than expected, pushing his way through overhanging branches and finding himself in the sunshine once again and on the reed-choked right bank of a slow moving stream that must have been about 20 cubits wide. Moving along the muddy bank, in and out of the sun through heavy growth, he was intrigued as tree frogs and marsh frogs scurried for cover. Birds screeched what sounded like warnings and flapped their way noisily into flight. Others sang and chirped in apparent unconcern. A dragonfly buzzed past his face and settled safely on the slow running water, glittering green and blue and silver in the reflecting light.

Jesus watched it in delight. He wanted to touch it. No, that wasn't it at all. He wanted to *be* the dragonfly. He wanted to experience what the dragonfly was experiencing, to know what the dragonfly knew.

Sitting down on a large, moss-covered rock at the water's edge, he removed one sandal and then the other, not taking his eye off the dragonfly as the water carried it in a slow, almost imperceptible circle.

Then he stood, pulled the strap of his knapsack from his shoulder, set the knapsack on top of his sandals, and pulled his tunic up over his head. The mud felt good oozing between his toes, and he lingered to enjoy it before extending his left foot out into the water and easing it onto the gravel bottom. Then the right—carefully so as not to alarm the dragonfly—and the left again. The water was cool and up to his knees now. He took another step, this time exploring with his toes as he searched for good footing. And another. On the stream's gently swirling surface the iridescent dragonfly was lazily circling back toward him.

Jesus squinted in the afternoon glare, the sun baking against his bare back. The clear water of life rippled gently against his thighs. As in a dream, he gazed downward at his feet beneath the surface—undulating, distorting, mesmerizing—not *his* feet at all but those of a shadowed figure that loomed above him in the brilliance of the day. He was the dragonfly, lulled into drifting, purposeless indolence, watching without concern a motionless silhouette against a blinding sky. His knees released and slowly he slipped lower in the water, allowing it to cover his waist, his chest, his shoulders, the ends of his hair now floating and spreading on the surface as he took a deep breath, wrapped his arms about his knees, and let himself be lifted by the water, encompassed by the water, nourished by the water.

He drifted, weightless, his back still warmed by the sun.

"Repent, for the kingdom of heaven is at hand!" The voice exploded from somewhere that seemed to be everywhere.

Isolated in time and space, he remained motionless, still drifting idly, still enveloped by the clear water, still resonating with the all-encompassing peace of being a Not-Self within the Not-Self that was the dragonfly. For a moment—for an eternity—he held on to his awareness beyond awareness, only gradually acknowledging the altering state of his consciousness. *Repent!* Float. Drift. Bask. *Repent!* At some point he raised his head, releasing his hold on his knees and allowing them to rest on the gritty sand that was the bottom of the stream while he lifted his head and let his attention refocus: water, trees, heat, a squawking crow overhead. Eventually he turned around completely, raising one hand to shield his eyes and looking back to the spot where he'd entered the water.

The man was partially kneeling on the same rock that Jesus had used while removing his sandals. Tangled hair, unkempt beard, and bushy eyebrows gave the stranger a wild, almost desperate appearance, an appearance magnified by the tunic of camel's hair that he wore and the leather belt about his waist. Standing behind him, tall and thin, was a young man whose long blond hair and wispy beard suggested a vulnerable fragility in stark contrast to the lion of a man who was kneeling.

Jesus smiled.

"Make ready the way of the Lord!" the lion roared. "Make His paths straight!"

"Isaiah," Jesus said.

"John," the man growled.

"The words," Jesus attempted to clarify. "The words are from Isaiah. 'Make ready the way of the Lord.'" He shifted his attention to the young man standing behind John and smiled again.

The young man smiled uncertainly in return.

"Andrew," John said. "That's Andrew," he repeated when Jesus looked back at him questioningly.

Jesus nodded, turned in the water to see if the dragonfly was still floating, experiencing a strange sense of loss when he realized that the insect was no longer present.

"I don't suppose you saw the Dove," John said from behind him.

With his hand still partially submerged, Jesus squeezed his fingers against his palm to create a series of squirts in the direction of where the dragonfly had been. The question seemed irrelevant.

"Or the heavens open up," John added.

Jesus turned lazily in the water and made eye contact with Andrew, raising his eyebrows questioningly.

Andrew raised his eyebrows in return.

By this time, John had stood up and moved ankle deep into the water. "Raise your eyebrows all you want," he scolded petulantly. "While you were baptizing yourself, the Spirit descended, right out of the sun, in the form of a dove and hovered over you."

Baptizing himself? "Didn't notice," Jesus said. "My head was under water." He stood up and ran his fingers backwards along his scalp to force some of the water out of his hair. A chorus of twittering, singing, calling birds in the surrounding trees abruptly broke into his consciousness.

For a moment, John stood silently contemplating Jesus. "I don't suppose you heard the voice either," he said at last.

Jesus looked at him, studying this man whom they called a prophet, before shaking his head and moving toward his clothing on the bank. "Not sure," he said. "I heard someone say 'Repent'. I've been assuming that was you."

"That *was* me," John said. He moved back to pick up Jesus' tunic and hand it to him. "That was *after* the voice came out of the heavens."

Jesus accepted the tunic, pushing his arms through the sleeves and pulling the garment over his head as he spoke. "A voice came out of the heavens," he repeated. "You'd think I'd have noticed." He sat on the rock and pushed one foot into a sandal.

"Andrew heard it!" John said, twisting to look at his companion. "Tell the man what the voice said."

Still holding one sandal, Jesus looked up at Andrew's face. A voice from heaven! Scripture spoke of such things. The Lord communicated with men all the time: Noah, Abraham, Jacob, Moses. Why *not* a voice from heaven?

"I'm not sure I heard it," Andrew said apologetically. "I think maybe you have to be a prophet in order to hear the Lord's voice."

"Thou art my beloved son!" John roared. "Thou art my beloved son! In thee I am well-pleased!" He splashed back into the water, wading to the middle of the stream and turning back to face Jesus before slapping his huge open hand on the surface of the water. "Right here!" he shouted, slapping the water again. "The dove descended to this spot! The voice was talking to you!" He repeated the sentence again, thundering each word separately to emphasize his point. "Thou...art...my...beloved...son!" Another punishing slap.

"I'll take your word for it." He hadn't intended the words to be sarcastic, but he heard the skepticism and knew that John must hear it as well.

"Take *God's* word," John replied, his manner abruptly subdued but, if anything, more intense than when he'd been shouting. He moved toward Jesus until they were standing face to face. "My word is nothing. After me, one is coming who is mightier than I, and I am not fit to stoop down and untie the thong of his sandals." His fiery eyes burned their way through Jesus' neutrality.

"My friend," Jesus said, returning burning gaze for burning gaze, "I do not question that you have heard God." He broke eye contact to turn his head toward Andrew. "As has Andrew." He reached down to pick up his knapsack and pulled the strap onto his shoulder before taking a few steps upward through the tall grass and then turning to look back at John. The words were poised on his lips, but he let them die there, unspoken. "God does not speak to us in a booming voice from the sky but in the intense whispering of our souls." He turned and moved through the overhanging branches back along the path he'd followed from the perimeter of the wadi.

"His winnowing fork is in his hand!" John roared after him. "He'll gather the wheat into his barn and burn up the chaff with unquenchable fire!"

2

The first crack of the weighted, braided leather thongs against his back is enough to weaken his resolve, yet somehow he manages not to cry out—not on the first or second… How many have there been? Has there been a tenth or fifteenth? A 20th, 30th, 39th? He doesn't know. It is only now—now that the lictor is leaning over him, gently pressing two fingers to the side of his throat—that he becomes aware of the viscid blood that covers his naked body, of the acidic, fetid odor that envelops him. It is only now that he can dully acknowledge the awful pain of the shredded, hanging flesh and muscle of his back and legs.

For reasons that he could not explain even to himself, Jesus found himself again in the wilderness as the sun disappeared behind the mountains at his back. He considered the possibility that he'd directed his steps into this desolate area because it was here that Moses and the Israelites had camped for months before crossing into the Promised Land. It was near here, the Scriptures taught, that Elijah, upon God's command, had sought refuge and was fed meat and bread by the ravens every morning and evening. It was here, as well, that the Lord had sent a chariot of fire and horses of fire to transport Elijah to heaven.

These were good stories. Jesus had grown up hearing them and believing them and fearing the God who made them true. At the same time, he'd come to know that, in spite of the truth these stories held, they were stories about events that probably had never happened. It was this truth, though, that beckoned him. It was the truth of John's vision of the sky opening and the dove descending that held him. It was the truth of the messiah who would deliver the people from their oppressors that now brought him to this dark, forbidding place. As he lay on the cold, rocky ground on this moonless night, gazing upward at the stars defining the earthly limits, he found himself thinking, not of spiritual matters, but of the food and comfort and camaraderie that he might instead be enjoying in the cave of John the Baptist. He thought of spiny mice and vipers dancing their nightly dance of survival. He let his mind drift through the events of the day. The night enveloped him.

"If you are the Son of God," the Adversary said to him, "tell this stone to become bread."

Jesus sat up with a start. Had he been sleeping? The night was still dark and the stars still bright. There was no sign in the western sky that dawn was near. If it had been a dream, he would have been dreaming about water, not about bread. His thirst was already sucking his stomach dry.

The Son of God? It was John's fault. "Thou art my beloved son," John's God had said. What could that possibly mean? It was nonsense. In the dream, had he responded to the Adversary? Dreams were elusive. He was pretty certain that there had been no response from him. But if he'd answered, what might he have said? He stared toward the dark shapes that were the western mountains. "Man shall not live on bread alone," he spoke aloud. "Man shall not live on bread alone." Meaning what? Meaning, maybe, "I'd rather have a drink of water." It was a good enough response from Yeshua ben Yusuf, but it was totally inadequate from the Son of God. Basically, the response was irrelevant. The Adversary had been testing him, challenging him. That was the Adversary's job. How marvelous would it be to be able to feed the poor by turning rocks into bread. That was what a loving God would do for his people: ease their hunger, relieve their suffering.

He lay back onto the uneven ground and closed his eyes. How long was this night going to be? What had he been thinking? But that was the thing, wasn't it. He *hadn't* been thinking. He'd left the comfort of the wadi and headed into the wilderness for no rational reason. If he was lucky, he could empty his mind and sleep through the rest of the night. He'd done it before. The trick was to focus on his heartbeat: pulsing steadily, warmly, dispassionately.

He was standing on the pinnacle of the temple in the holy city on Mount Moriah. It was on this mountain that Abraham had offered Isaac as a sacrifice. It was here that Solomon had built the first temple. To his right, Mount Zion rose into the darkness above the Valley of Hinnom, the "abhorred place". On the pinnacle Jesus shivered and shifted his gaze to his left where the Kidron Valley separated Mount Moriah from the higher Mount of Olives. Beyond that the land dropped down rapidly to the River Jordan.

"If you are the Son of God, throw yourself down." The Adversary was behind him in the shadow of the pinnacle.

"I am not the Son of God." Jesus heard his own voice as a hollow, distorted echo.

"Throw yourself down," the Adversary repeated, "for it is written, 'He will give his angels charge concerning you, and on their hands they will bear you up.'"

This time Jesus was not startled into wakefulness. This time he'd almost been expecting the dream. This time he let himself linger on the pinnacle, somehow both in the dream and out of it simultaneously. He was able to control it, to consider a response to the Adversary's direction, to live the illusion even as he knew himself to be lying on his back in the wilderness. "On the other hand," Jesus heard himself responding, "it is written, 'You shall not put the Lord your God to the test.'"

He let his eyes open slowly to the starlit sky, intentionally declaring his separation from the scene atop the pinnacle. In his dream he had spoken the words, but they were not his own. They were words that everyone knew, not because they were written—after all, how many men could read?—but because they were true. Well, *accepted* as true. So, in the dream, had he spoken truth or had he spoken dogma? Were the scriptures the word of God or the word of men speaking for God? Either way, it seemed to make sense. Challenging the Lord could never be a good idea. On the other hand, how could any man ever understand the distinction: if he was challenging or acknowledging?

A stone was pressing into the small of his back, and he twisted to reach under himself to remove it. The effort was only partially successful. Now other stones imposed themselves on his consciousness.

So what was happening here? Where did dreams come from? Was his mind simply cavorting while he slept? Was his imagination just enjoying itself, twisting and turning his waking experiences to examine them from different points of view? Or was something outside himself, some cosmic reality—God—attempting to teach him a universal truth? Was God speaking to him?

He took a deep breath, pushed thoughts of thirst and cool water from his mind, and closed his eyes. He could do this. He could endure the discomfort of this night. He could get back to sleep and let sleep transport him magically to sunrise. By mid-morning he would be back in John's watery thicket, his stomach full, his thirst quenched, his body cleansed. He took himself there now, drifting lazily with the dragonfly, floating, circling, warmed by the brilliance of the sun.

From among the stars he could look down and see himself sleeping in the wilderness. He could see the Jordan winding eternally between the mountains. Beyond that, to the east, Arabia and Mesopotamia stretched endlessly. Rippling white waves of the great sea moved relentlessly toward the surrounding shores: Italy, Achaia, Asia, Syria, Egypt, Africa.

He was not alone on this celestial mountain. Beside him—not so much beside him as all around him—a shadow, a living, undulating darkness hovered. "All these things I will give you," the darkness said.

Jesus turned his head to question the darkness.

"All these things I will give you," the darkness repeated, "if you fall down and worship me."

"These things are not yours to give," Jesus said. He turned to escape the darkness, to marvel again at the glory of the earth spread out before him, but the darkness was now obscuring all. "There is only God," Jesus said to the Adversary who was the darkness who was Jesus himself.

And the darkness dissipated. And Jesus opened his eyes. And the golden glow of sunrise was spreading itself across the sky above the shadowed mountains to the west.

3

It is only a short distance from the Preatorium to Golgotha. How odd! Had it really been only a few months earlier? Tishri...the Festival of Booths...they'd come down through Samaria... But this day—this final day—the journey has seemed endless. The weight of the rough beam strapped across his shoulders again forces Jesus down. He sinks to the ground, hardly noticing the stones that cut into his bloody knees. Head bowed, he tenses, anticipating the inevitable derisive shouts and heavy blows from the guards.

"Maybe the end is not near," Jesus said matter-of-factly. "Maybe it is only the beginning."

John grunted in disgust and shook his tangled hair in apparent frustration. "This is impossible," he grumbled. "The people exist at the edge of death. The priests are corrupt. Not only is no one observing the Law, no one can even agree what the Law means." He stood up from the rock he'd been sitting on and turned to gaze westward across the green expanse that sloped downward toward the Jordan. "And the long awaited messiah sits on a rock in the shade of a tree and tells me that the end is not near."

Jesus smiled in the direction of Andrew and his brother Simon, who were sitting with him in front of John's cave. Two large musht, cleaned and boned, sizzled over a charcoal fire. Behind the brothers, the rocky, cave-pocked hill rose toward the wilderness. "Are you waiting for the messiah, Simon?" he asked.

Simon's square, weathered face was stoical. Only a slight pinching of his eyebrows and narrowing of his gaze gave any indication that he'd heard the question. His reply was a shrug of the shoulders.

"Of course he is!" John shouted, turning to face Jesus. "Everyone is waiting! The Pharisees and Sadducees come to the Jordan to be baptized. Even those vipers know that the end is near. They come to be purified and ready and then go back to Judea to cheat the people as always."

Jesus gestured for John to sit down and watched as the big man reluctantly did so. "And when the messiah comes," Jesus persisted, "that will be the end?"

"I baptize with water," John said defensively. "The one who is coming will baptize with the holy spirit and fire."

"Those who have not repented will be incinerated," Andrew added.

John grunted in affirmation.

"And then what?" Jesus asked, switching his gaze from John to Andrew to Simon.

"And then what?" John repeated.

Jesus focused his attention on John's face but said nothing, letting the question hang in the air.

"Then," John said, his voice now subdued, "then the Lord will bless those who remain. Then mankind will fear the Lord and keep his commandments."

"The Lord will let his people prosper," Andrew added. "Their cattle will thrive and their fields will produce in abundance."

"The fish will fill my nets every morning," Simon said with a grin.

Jesus waited to see if anyone had something more to add, examining the small entrance to John's cave, watching a line of migrating herons heading north over the river, listening to the gurgle of water passing from one level to another in a nearby pool. It seemed certain to him that the suffering of men is not the penalty inflicted by an angry God. He couldn't believe that the Lord curses his people for being what he has made it possible for them to be. It seemed ridiculous to believe that the Lord would reward his people for being victims.

He examined the faces of the three men there beside him, not certain what to say. It was almost that he, along with John and Andrew and Simon, was a listener.

The kingdom of heaven is not a place, his mind was silently insisting. The kingdom of heaven is not a status achieved through conflict or domination or cataclysmic events. The kingdom of heaven is not a condition made available to some but not to others. The messiah, should he ever come, would arrive, not amid flames of death but lifted by wings of Peace. For most, Jesus was certain, the messiah would glide through their lives unnoticed, like the group of herons that had passed overhead a moment ago.

Water whispered over ancient rocks. Crows squawked warnings to distant family members. The wings of insect multitudes hummed in electric harmony.

"The kingdom of heaven," Jesus heard himself begin, struggling to express a point that seemed always just out of reach. "*The kingdom of heaven is like a person who had a treasure hidden in his field but didn't know it. When he died, he left the fallow land to his son. The son didn't know about the treasure either. He took over the field and sold it. The buyer went plowing, discovered the treasure, and began to lend money at interest to whomever he wished.*"

An uneasy silence fell upon the three listeners. Jesus shifted uncomfortably on the rock where he was sitting and looked from man to man for signs that one might have understood the point of the story.

"The Law forbids lending money at interest," John argued sullenly, his usually powerful voice almost inaudible.

Jesus nodded. John was correct. The end of the story invalidated the point he'd been trying to make. At the same time, the irony of the situation amused him. How typically human! A man who discovers the treasure of God defiles the blessing by using it for personal profit.

"Nobody lets good land lie fallow," Andrew observed.

"It's a story," Simon argued. "The field had to be neglected or there wouldn't be any story. Where's your imagination?"

"There's nothing wrong with my imagination," Andrew answered. "The story just doesn't make sense."

John looked at Andrew with a condescending smile. "The buyer is the messiah," he said. "The treasure is purity."

"Purity," Jesus repeated, intrigued by John's unwavering sense of purpose.

John nodded, his eyes now locked intensely with those of Jesus. "There should have been a heavy rain in the story. The soil was washed away and the treasure revealed."

"Baptism!" Andrew said.

John looked at him across the gray coals of the fire and grinned. "The father who died and the son who sold the land were left unclean and destitute." He looked back at Jesus and raised his eyebrows victoriously.

Jesus closed his eyes. If he was going to use stories to communicate this message of God's kingdom—any message that might explode into existence in his soul—he was going to have to expect setbacks. A lot of people were going to miss the point. There was no way around it. People understood repentance. They understood an angry, vengeful God. They understood the need for immutable laws and the penalties for violating those laws. But they were not going to understand a God whose only instruction was to love your neighbor and who offered Peace right here, right now, to anyone who could live according to that credo. For that matter, Jesus had to admit, he didn't understand it very well himself.

John's bellow brought Jesus out of his reverie. "Are you guys going to eat those fish or just incinerate them!"

Simon got up and examined their sizzling breakfast. "Perfect," he scoffed. "Don't try to tell a fisherman how to cook fish."

"Locusts and wild honey," Andrew laughed. "If it weren't for insects, John would starve."

"Not so," John argued. He patted his stomach. "You don't get a belly like this on a diet of locusts. I eat whatever the Lord provides. If he doesn't provide, I don't eat."

Jesus stood up and moved to John's side, putting his arm around the big man's shoulders. "By any chance," he asked, "did the Lord provide a loaf of bread and a skin of wine to go with that fish?"

4

Through sweat-fogged eyes he watches in detachment as two legionnaires take the beam he'd been carrying and nail it across a longer beam lying on the barren ground. Within moments he is grabbed under the arms from behind, dragged to the crossed beams, and thrown backwards with his shoulders against the wood, his head thunking heavily against what would be the upright beam.

It seems to Jesus that these anonymous attendants are being almost gentle as they carefully position his arms so that his hands rest palms down on top of the crosspiece. But it is not about being gentle, he knows. It is about breathing. It is about being able to lift his body to relieve the pressure on his lungs. If he cannot exhale, he will mercifully suffocate within minutes. Crucifixion is not about mercy.

"How did you do that?" Andrew asked.

Jesus squinted past the blocks of dark stone houses of Capernaum into the glare reflecting off the sea beyond, replaying in his mind the events that had just taken place inside the synagogue. He'd been teaching. Nothing new about that. He'd been teaching in the synagogues of Galilee for several weeks now, ever since Simon, Andrew, and he had made the trek north from John's thicket in Bethany Beyond the Jordan.

"Casting out a demon on the sabbath," Simon groaned. "It doesn't matter how he did it. We're all in big trouble."

Jesus continued to stare at the water. At this time of day the sea was empty of the fishing boats that would begin setting their nets in the evening. "A lot of people with terrible demons these days, Simon," he said. "The demon of poverty." He turned his head to look at the big man next to him. "The demon of oppression. The demon of hopelessness." He put his arm around Simon's shoulder and looked up into the big man's eyes. "Any day is a good day to get rid of a demon," he said.

Simon appeared to consider that point of view. "But the sabbath," he argued weakly. "The Law forbids..."

"The sabbath was made for man," Jesus interrupted, *"not man for the sabbath."*

The statement didn't seem to turn on any lights for Simon, so Jesus tried a different tack. "Do you really think, Simon..." He removed his arm from his friend's shoulder and turned to sweep the others' faces so as to include them all. "...do you think that the Lord cares what day it is?" He paused to let that thought sink in before continuing. "Do you think that this tiny society of ours is all there is? What about Egypt? Macedonia? Gaul? What about those lands and those peoples beyond the world we know? The Roman Empire stretches to lands that you and I can't even imagine, and do you know what's at the limit of the Empire?" Again he paused to examine the face of each man present. "Beyond the Empire are seas and lands and people that even Romans can't imagine. Can we pretend that God doesn't care about those lands, about those people? Can we believe that God will punish them because they plow their land or sell their goods—or cast out demons—on the sabbath?"

No one in the group seemed inclined to respond, and Jesus allowed his attention to settle again on the sparkling water beyond them.

"The man was possessed by an actual demon," Nathanael insisted sullenly. "We heard the spirit speak."

Simon looked at him questioningly, a look that said, "What the heck do you know about it?" Then he looked to Jesus for confirmation. After all, Nathanael and Philip had been with Jesus for only a few days.

"Maybe," Jesus agreed.

"You told the demon to get out of him," Simon pointed out. "You must have thought there was a real demon."

"*He* thought there was a real demon," Jesus answered. "That's what matters."

"Screams. Threats. Convulsions." Nathanael insisted. "That wasn't a demon?"

Jesus stared past the young man and focused on the calm water beyond. "What is a demon, Nathanael?" He held his focus on the sea. "Where does it come from? Where does it go when it leaves? Why did it invade that man's body and not yours or Philip's?"

"It's a messenger of Satan," Philip offered.

"It's Satan himself," Nathanael corrected.

Jesus took Nathanael's arm and began leading him down the steps toward the street. "And Satan is?"

Nathanael stopped. "The Lord is good," he answered matter-of-factly. "Satan is evil."

Jesus pulled at his arm so that they could continue to the street. "So, then," he said, "there must be two Gods, one good and one evil. Right?"

Simon hurried past them, stopping when he reached the bottom step. "Teacher," he said almost in a hush, "you're talking blasphemy. You're speaking the name of God."

Jesus grinned. "'God' isn't God's name, Simon," he said. "And 'Satan' certainly is not his name either."

"So," Nathanael said, "you're telling us that Satan doesn't exist and demons don't exist. That man in the synagogue was just crazy."

"It's *you* who say that," Jesus answered. "All I've done is ask questions." He reached out and turned Simon in the direction of his house. "We'll have to talk about demons one day soon," he said, putting a little pressure on Simon's back to get him moving. "Right now, I'm starving."

Simon began moving rapidly along the narrow street that ran between the blocks of houses, turning to call back to the others as they followed. "My wife has dinner ready," he said. "My mother-in-law isn't feeling well, but we can eat outside in the courtyard."

"What's the matter with her?" Philip called after him.

"Don't know," Simon said. "Fever. Headache. Trouble breathing. She just lies on her mat and doesn't say much.

"Are James and John going to be there?" Jesus asked as Simon hurried ahead.

"I think so," Simon called over his shoulder. "Zebedee needed them to mend nets. Told them fishing for men was okay for prophets but fishing for fish put food on the table."

Fishing for men. That was the phrase he'd used, surely enough. It seemed witty at the time—almost profound. In retrospect, however, Zebedee was correct: it was nonsense. What they were doing now was nothing like fishing. The fishermen of Galilee laid down their trammel nets in darkness and pulled them in at first light, hoping to find them full of musht that came in from the deep water to feed in the shallows during the night. Jesus and his... What were they: friends, companions, workers? They were all of those things, but more. They believed in him. They embraced his message of Peace and Equality. They were passionate to spread the message to others, to anyone who would listen.

Disciples! They were disciples. And there were no fish involved in what they were trying to do; no one got caught up in a net. Instead of moving from life to death, disciples hoped to move people from death to life.

He followed the others into a courtyard, an open area surrounded on three sides by houses, including Simon's. Near each doorway was a fire pit where women tended fish being grilled. Near the center of the courtyard was a large community oven where bread was being baked.

"Jesus," Simon called from one corner of the courtyard. He was standing with his arm around a young woman. "Come over and meet my wife."

Jesus waved and moved toward them, having to move through the group of men who had just entered ahead of him.

"Perpetua, this is our teacher," Simon told his wife. "John the Baptist calls him the Son of God."

Jesus playfully put the palm of his hand over Simon's mouth. "John the Baptist has been known to exaggerate," he said, smiling at Perpetua.

"You should have seen what happened at the synagogue," Simon continued. "He drove a demon out of a man."

Not that again.

"Can I speak with your mother?" Jesus asked Perpetua, eager to change the subject.

Perpetua hesitated. "She's sick," she told him apologetically.

He nodded. "Simon told us," he said.

Simon didn't want to let go of the demon story. "There's no point in being modest, Teacher," he grinned. "Everyone in Capernaum is going to know. They probably already know."

Jesus gave him a pat on the rear and followed Perpetua into the shadowed house. In the far corner of the room, he could see where the old woman lay on her mat. He walked to her, standing over her silently for perhaps a minute until she opened her eyes and acknowledged his presence. Then he sat down cross-legged on the floor, aware that Perpetua had moved away and left the two of them alone. He was conscious, as well, of the loud voices of the people outside in the courtyard. The heat and heavy air of the room lay upon him, the foul stench of illness seeming to permeate even the stone walls themselves as the woman's chest rose and fell in a resigned struggle to breathe. Jesus closed his eyes and allowed himself to be consumed by her strength of will, existing within it, transported by it beyond the noise and heat and stench into silence and coolness and purity. Without any conscious effort on his part, his open hand moved in a sweeping, cleansing, gathering dance above the woman's breast.

It was her voice that startled him into awareness. "I'm feeling better," she said.

He opened his eyes and looked into hers.

"I've got to get up and help Perpetua with the meal," she said as she struggled into a sitting position.

Jesus smiled but made no effort to assist her. "Are you sure?" he asked.

With considerable effort, she stood up. "No, I'm not sure," she said. "But I should be helping." She coughed, a hard, grinding cough that could not possibly have helped to clear her chest. She began walking toward the doorway.

Jesus got to his feet and followed, giving Perpetua a lifted eyebrow as her mother walked past her into the courtyard. He leaned and spoke quietly into her ear. "She says she's feeling better," he said.

"What did you do?" Perpetua asked, looking not at him but at her mother, who had already ordered Simon away from the fire and begun to turn the fish on the grill.

"Pray, maybe?" Jesus said. "I'm not sure. If I was praying, I don't remember what I said."

"You healed her!" Perpetua exclaimed in a voiceless but powerful whisper.

Before he could protest, she hurried from his side and went to Simon, who was now standing with Andrew and the others. Jesus watched as she spoke to her husband and then turned to gaze back at him. All of them were staring at him. He felt the need to deny and clarify but knew that there would be nothing he could say to change their minds. Simon's mother-in-law had been too sick to even be on her feet, and now she was up and functioning. There was no rational way to explain it. The Son of God talk was nonsense. John's vision of the dove descending from heaven could not possibly have been anything more than delusion. Yeshua ben Yusuf was human, totally and unmistakably human. It was impossible to consider any other possibility. Still, there was no way to avoid acknowledging that there was something very different about him. For some inexplicable reason, he understood what other men did not understand. Incredibly, God seemed to be working through him to change the way men lived their lives. The messiah? Hardly. There would be no messiah who, in an explosion of cosmic power, would save humankind from itself. But it was conceivable—it was even logical—that there would be a messenger, a teacher who might help individual humans to know God's purpose for them.

"Teacher!" Simon was moving toward him. "A family just arrived. Their small son has a twisted leg. They're asking you to heal him."

"Simon!" Jesus answered, controlling his anger only with difficulty. "I can't heal a twisted leg! No one can heal a twisted leg!"

Simon's expression changed from elation to disappointment. "Teacher," he said, a hopeful smile forming again as he spoke, "please try. We believe in you."

Jesus looked toward the family at the gate and then at the group of...disciples gazing at him quietly. "I can talk to them about the kingdom of heaven," he told Simon. "I can help them be at peace with their son's condition."

Simon nodded, glanced over his shoulder at his wife, and then looked back at Jesus and grinned. "That'll be good," he said, taking Jesus' arm and pulling him gently toward the waiting family.

Jesus took two or three steps and then stopped. "Simon," he insisted quietly, "after I've spoken with this family…"

Simon was staring into Jesus' eyes intently, almost adoringly.

"…after I've spoken with this family, I've got to have a cup of wine and something to eat."

Simon grinned and gave him a gentle punch in the shoulder. "You got it," he said. "I'll serve you myself."

5

A shrill, piercing scream explodes silently in his mind as a heavy, square, wrought iron nail is driven through his left wrist and into the wood of the crosspiece. Anticipating the second nail in his right wrist, he attempts to steel himself, to deny the horror of a second scream even as the first still reverberates in his soul.

The nail is driven and the second scream shatters his resolve, its intensity energized anew with each blow of the hammer.

His left leg is flexed slightly and his foot is placed at the side of the cross. A third nail is driven with a fiery explosion of pain through the heel and into the wood. Then the legionnaire moves to the right leg, flexes it carefully, and drives a final nail through the heel of the right foot.

An early light that was not yet light enabled Jesus to pick his way through the deserted streets of Capernaum and then beyond toward the spot where the sun would rise over the hills to the east. He kept to the rocky shoreline, knowing that his destination was the Jordan where it emptied into the sea but not really thinking about where he was going. His mind, instead, was focused on the events of the night before. By sundown, with the sabbath officially ended, the line of people at the gate seeking his help had stretched down the street toward the synagogue. The situation was impossible. Even with his disciples to assist in maintaining order, the crowd had become impatient. Why should it take so long for the Son of God to heal a tumor, to restore eyesight, to eliminate pain? A wave of the hand, they believed, a touch of his garment, a word from his lips would be all it would take.

For a while he'd tried to be the healer they believed him to be. He'd moved down the line, speaking to each person, laying his hand… Oh, my God! The man in the shadows, calling his name, coming up to him and falling on his knees. The people moving back in panic, pushing and shoving one another to get clear, women screaming, men shouting threats against the life of this outcast. "If you are willing," the poor man begged, "you can make me clean." If he was willing? Of course he was willing? But what could he do?

Jesus had peered at the leper as best he could through the poor light. The man hadn't seemed to be deformed. Granted, his garments covered most of his body, but there was nothing obvious to identify him as unclean: no oozing sores, no hideous misshaping of his face, no putrid odors emanating from his person. Still, the people were in a frenzy of fear. Inevitably the crowd was going to get out of control and there could be serious injuries.

And so he'd reached down and laid his hand against the leper's leathery cheek, holding it there, keenly aware of the life force being exchanged between cheek and hand, soul and soul. And time had stood still. Place had ceased to exist. Honor and shame and social status had dissipated.

When he'd dropped his hand at last, a viable, permeating quiet had settled over the scene. Only an undulating glow from the cooking fires in the courtyard and a few dancing flames from torches along the street broke the stillness. The leper had risen unsteadily, scanned the line of shadowy people hesitantly, and then shuffled slowly up the street, anonymous, unremarkable, healed yet unhealed.

The barren hills in the distance were now silhouetted against the brilliance of the sun rising beyond them. Not far ahead, the clear water of the Jordan, having completed only about a third of its journey from the peak of Mount Hermon, would be slowing and widening through the low wetlands as it approached the sea. Anticipating this, Jesus turned to his left and worked his way to higher ground before turning east again toward the upper river where he would be able to establish himself in the shade of a tamarisk and sort out the events of the past several weeks.

Had he healed the leper? Yes and no. In all probability, the man had awakened this morning with the same skin sores he'd had yesterday. If the Lord wanted to heal sores or flaking, scaly skin, he didn't need any help from Jesus. As uncomfortable and unsightly as those conditions might be, it was not really the physical reality that made the man anathema. He was unclean because he was different, not because he was contagious. He was untouchable, not because his sores might infect another person but because those accepted by the community did not have such sores. By laying his hand upon the leper, Jesus had not healed the disease, he had healed the ostracism. He had invited the man into the community.

He could hear the river now. He hurried his pace through the underbrush toward the grove of tamarisks. Not surprisingly, he thought of the little thicket of John the Baptist. Unlike John's serene pools and slow moving stream, the Jordan at this point was rushing past powerfully, but the peace was the same. Here he could listen, not only to the birds and to the rushing water, but to the universe, whose message was always available but too often lost in the confusion of living.

The image of John standing at the edge of the pool in the lower Jordan now formed itself in Jesus' mind. Not strange, really, that such a man would be taken into custody. Not strange that this man of the Law would be seen as a threat to Herod, even to Tiberius. Repent, John had said. Baptize yourself and prepare for the coming of the Messiah. Men of power would not appreciate such a message. Eliminating the messenger is hardly an original approach to dealing with those who raise their voice in protest.

And what about his own voice? *Don't react violently against the one who is evil: when someone slaps you on the right cheek, turn the other as well. When someone wants to sue you for your shirt, let that person have your coat along with it. When someone conscripts you for one mile, go an extra mile. Give to the one who begs from you. If you have money, don't lend it at interest. Rather, give it to someone from whom you won't get it back.* Nothing threatening about that message. Not likely that those in power would find it necessary to eliminate Yeshua ben Yusuf. Even the priests of the Temple could hardly find fault.

He had to admit, however, that every message could be twisted and misinterpreted. Almost every town he entered provided someone eager to trip him up, eager to get him in trouble with authorities. A week or two earlier, he'd given his usual statement in support of those who live in poverty: "*Congratulations to the poor,*" he'd said, "*for to you belongs heaven's domain.*" A man among the listeners, probably someone who'd learned to work the system to his great advantage, tried to trick him into taking the next step. Should the poor have to pay the poll tax to the Roman emperor, he wanted to know? It was pleasing now under the tree beside the Jordan for Jesus to replay the scene in his mind. He'd asked the man for a coin, and when he'd been handed a silver coin, he pretended to examine it and then held it up and asked whose picture was on it, whose name was on it. Of course the man had replied that the image was that of the emperor. "*Pay the emperor what belongs to the emperor,"* he'd replied, *"and God what belongs to God."*

No, there was no reason to fear that he would meet the same fate as John, but this did not mean that he should not be fearful. There was much to fear. First and foremost was the very real danger that the people would see him as God incarnate. His purpose could not be one of offering the people quick fixes. Presuming to cure illness and to exorcise demons was little more than a side show. Plenty of self-proclaimed wizards and spiritists already feasted on the people's desperation. Comforting the sick was one thing. Promising miraculous healing was quite another.

He lay back and closed his eyes, allowing the roar of the rushing water to envelop him. Reluctantly he allowed his mind to take him back to last night: to the boy with the twisted leg, to the leper, to the endless cue of human misery. Each individual, each family unit had a story—in one sense, the same story, yet each different and personal and tragic. Now, alone beneath the cooling spread of the tamarisks, he could dwell on each, replay each conversation in his mind, marvel over and over again at the peace that descended over them all at his touch. What was happening? Was he helping or making things worse by giving them false hope? Injury by injury, disease by disease, defect by defect, he remembered...regretted...speculated.

"Teacher!"

The call reached him through a fog of sleep.

"Teacher!"

He was awake now, groggily attempting to reorient himself—the relentless rush of the river, the hard ground beneath his back, the sinking recollection of overwhelming responsibility.

"Teacher!" The voice was closer now and unmistakably Simon's.

Jesus sat up and turned to look back along the route he'd followed to reach this place. Simon, Andrew, James...it looked like all of the six plus several he didn't recognize had come to find him. Perpetua was with them, as well, and another young woman he didn't know. He waved and stood up, pleased to see them yet annoyed by what felt like an intrusion. He decided that the most sociable thing to do would be to walk back along the path and show pleasant surprise at their arrival. And why shouldn't he be pleasantly surprised? This was the nucleus of his army of peace. Army of Peace. The phrase had a nice ring to it. Maybe even John the Baptist would have bought into that image.

He survived a bear hug from Simon and exchanged more moderate hugs with those he knew until he reached Perpetua. To her he held out his hand and smiled, pleased that she'd joined the men in seeking him. Even more pleasing were the two baskets that the women carried, baskets that more than likely would provide them all with sardines and bread for breakfast.

"Teacher, this is Mary," she said, returning his smile. "She's from Magdala. It didn't take long for word of your healing to reach them there. She left before first light to get to Capernaum."

He looked at Mary, uncertain what to say. Welcoming a young, beautiful woman to this group was not at all like dealing with a man. "You must be tired," he said, the words sounding stiff, almost unfriendly.

Mary grinned, clearly not in awe of him. "Two hours from my home to Simon's," she said. "Two more to this spot. That's not a difficult journey...even for a helpless woman."

"Don't buy that story, Teacher," Simon laughed. "Mary's about as helpless as an ibex on the side of a mountain."

"Simon," Perpetua scolded. "It's not very nice to compare Mary to a goat."

"She knows what I mean."

"I take it as a compliment," Mary insisted, her dark eyes fastened on Jesus. Her voice was husky, soothing like a heavy wine.

The moment felt awkward. Jesus looked over his shoulder toward the spot where he'd been sitting and then back at Mary. "Why don't we get out of the sun," he suggested as he turned and began walking toward the river.

He found a large, relatively flat rock in the shade and sat on it, motioning for the others to sit around him. "So," he began after everyone had settled themselves. "You found me."

No one seemed to feel the need to respond.

"I needed some time to myself," he added, still feeling oddly self-conscious. "I had to find a quiet place where I could hear what the Lord had to say to me."

"You were praying," Andrew said.

Jesus shifted his attention to Andrew briefly before cocking his head to one side and gazing over the heads of the group into the branches of the trees. "Maybe I was praying," he spoke to the branches. "I wasn't asking for anything. It was more like I was just letting the Lord take my thoughts wherever he wanted them to go."

The rush of the river below them abruptly dominated, somehow heightening the silence.

"Everyone was looking for you," Nathanael said.

Jesus looked past the spot where Nathanael sat. "Everyone," he repeated. "Everyone who wants something."

Nathanael nodded.

"That's why I came out here," Jesus said.

Philip had remained standing while the others sat, a stocky, beardless man with a hairline that had receded to the back of his head in spite of his relative youth. "Teacher," he said, his manner suggesting that he had an idea to sell. "It's a perfect situation. The word of your healing is already spreading throughout Galilee. People know that they can come to Capernaum and find you there. You don't have to go anywhere. We don't have to go anywhere. What better way to spread your message than to have people listen while they're still in awe of the miraculous cures you have to offer."

For some reason, Jesus looked to Mary for her reaction to the idea, disappointed that her expression was one of interest but not judgment. He let his eyes move deliberately from face to face. Mostly what he read in each face was enthusiasm. Possibly they'd already discussed this among themselves.

"It's a logical suggestion, Philip," he began, hearing in his words of apparent support, as Philip must also hear, the impending objection. "A broker." The term hung unpleasantly in the clear morning air. "You...Simon, James...could be my broker and I your client."

He watched Mary's eyebrows rise.

Philip looked around at the others before responding. "No," he said, "that's not the word I'd use."

Jesus studied Philip's face intently. "What word would you use?" he asked. "Manager? Scribe? Accountant?"

"That's not fair, Teacher," Simon broke in. "You're making us sound greedy."

"There wouldn't be any fees involved," Philip added. "It's just a practical way of handling what could otherwise be a very inefficient process. Why go out and spend a lot of time and effort finding people..."

"Who may or may not be interested," Nathanael interrupted.

Philip looked at Nathanael and nodded. "...when we can get people to come voluntarily to us?"

It was unrealistic to believe that money would not be involved, Jesus knew, but he chose not to argue the point. At the moment, these men had the best of intentions. Good intentions or not, however, they were missing the bigger picture. They could talk about the kingdom of heaven, but they weren't yet able to experience it. "And who would these people be?" he asked. "Who would be traveling long distances to listen to our message?"

"The people of Galilee," Philip replied. "Eventually, no doubt, from Judea, as well. Syria, Samaria, Decapolis...who knows? Anyone with problems..."

"And that's everyone," Simon interrupted again. "Anybody here who doesn't have problems?"

"...the miserable, downtrodden, oppressed people who are the very ones you hope to save," Philip finished. He looked around at the others for support.

"The tenant farmer," Jesus asked. "Will the landowner allow him to leave the fields to find me?"

Mary's eyes moved from Jesus to Philip.

"Beggars?" Jesus continued. "Criminals, outlaws, itinerant workers? A poverty stricken weaver from Jericho? Slaves? Shepherds and goatherds? The aged? The infirm? Women?"

John jumped up and silently extended both burly arms, palms up, in the direction of Mary.

"Mary doesn't count," James laughed. "She's an ibex."

Mary grinned and let the men guffaw and add their crude comments, the tension in her eyes belying the grin, making it clear that she was waiting for them to settle down, watching for an opportunity to respond, anticipating the awkward silence that would take the place of their boisterous maleness.

Jesus studied her face, the long, dark, uncovered hair, the glinting silver rings that dangled from her ears. He waited for her to speak; not surprisingly, he knew what she would say.

"In Magdala..." she began, her honeyed voice a counterpoint to the steady hum of life that filled the warmth of the morning. "...in Magdala we are fish processors. We salt the fish that Zebedee's boat, that Simon's boat—that an entire fleet of boats from the cooperatives—bring to us. The fish are transported to wealthy landowners, wealthy bureaucrats, wealthy governors, wealthy priests, wealthy scribes throughout Israel."

"That's an important list," Jesus broke in. "Those are the same people who would be arriving in Capernaum seeking me."

"To be healed?" John asked.

"A lot of them," Jesus replied.

"Why else?" Simon asked.

Jesus smiled but gave no answer. This was not the time to be talking about those who would be fearing his message, those who would be seeking to eliminate this threat to their status, this threat to tradition, this threat, as they perceived it, to their status as God's chosen people.

He looked at Mary and smiled. "Sorry to interrupt," he said.

"Salted fish are shipped as far away as Rome," she continued. "It's big business. A few people make a lot of money."

She paused to scan the group of men slowly, her dark eyes locking with those of Jesus for several seconds before flicking away and staring past him toward the river. "The list of wealthy does not include those who do the work," she continued finally. "The fish processors of Magdala exist in a living Sheol. They have no money. They have no time or energy for themselves or their family. They salt fish today. They salt fish tomorrow."

"They aren't going to walk five miles to Capernaum to be healed?" Nathanael asked.

Mary hesitated. "I don't think this is about healing," she said.

"Carp poop!" Philip scoffed.

Jesus grinned but didn't look at Philip. "Carp poop?" he repeated. It had a pithy jolt to it. Carp poop.

"Carp poop," Philip repeated. "People will go anywhere, do anything, to get rid of their pain. And that's *exactly* what this is about." There was a general murmur of assent as Philip turned and walked to the edge of the group and stared at the river below them.

Jesus watched Philip move, gazed past him for a moment through the speckled shade of the trees, and then lowered his eyes to study a trail of ants at his feet. What was he doing here, after all? It was all so hopeless. These were good men. These were men who believed that they understood his message, men who were willing to devote their lives to bringing that message to others, yet the fact was that they still didn't get it. Mary was right. This was not about healing. At the same time, it was all about healing. Not about escaping pain but about finding meaning, not about accumulating wealth but about embracing poverty, not about gaining power over others but about gaining power over self.

"The kingdom of God," he heard himself saying, "is not a broker society. In the kingdom of God, everyone belongs; everyone has access."

The trail of ants continued, each ant probably engrossed in its own survival, most likely not compassionate, most likely not concerned about its relationship with its fellow ants. But what about these men and women gathered with him this morning? It was their responsibility to love not only themselves but their family and friends and every other human being, even their enemies. Had he told these guys yet that they should *love their enemies*? If he hadn't, it was just as well. They'd consider such a thing impossible. Maybe they'd be right.

"God's imperial rule," he said without looking up, *"is like leaven which a woman took and concealed in 50 pounds of flour until it was all leavened."* He could almost hear the words repeating themselves in the minds of the disciples, reverberating, bouncing crazily against the interior walls of their skulls, endlessly defying every attempt to examine and make sense of them. Fifty pounds of flour is a lot of flour. Why would the woman conceal it? Inevitably it would do its work inside the flour no matter how well concealed it might be. Leaven is corrupt and evil. Unleavened bread is holy.

"Teacher?"

It was Simon, of course. He was the only one likely to admit that he didn't understand. Jesus raised his head, hoping the expression on his face was one of patience and encouragement.

"The parable doesn't make sense," Simon complained. "Doesn't make sense to me, I mean. I don't understand..."

"...how something corrupt can represent the kingdom of heaven," Jesus finished for him.

Simon nodded.

"Why does leaven have to be corrupt?" Mary asked. "What makes it evil? Leaven in dough makes the bread rise, gives it flavor. Does anyone here like unleavened bread?"

"Passover," Perpetua said, almost to herself.

Andrew picked up on the thought immediately. "The Israelites didn't have time to put leaven in their bread before escaping from Egypt."

"So?" Mary persisted. "We're not the Israelites. We've got time. God's got time." She reached into her basket, pulled out a loaf of bread, and tossed it to Andrew. "Try it," she laughed. "You'll like it."

John reached in front of the startled Andrew and intercepted the loaf. "Manna from heaven!" he shouted, holding it above his head and tearing it in two. One half he shared with James, mostly because James grabbed his arm and wrested that piece from his grasp. They both took big bites and chewed with exaggerated delight. This set off a playful scuffle as Simon attempted to take what remained of John's half.

"The kingdom of heaven tastes pretty damn fine!" James shouted, his mouth still full.

Mary threw a second loaf and a third. By this time Perpetua had joined her, and loaf after loaf was hurled into the midst of the laughing, shouting men as they jostled for position.

Jesus watched in amusement. This was a very good way to end a discussion that had become far too solemn. Talk about healing! These men were going to be laughing for the remainder of the morning. The return trek to Capernaum would be made with the sense that important matters had been settled. Tomorrow it would be easy to take his leave and allow these men to get back to earning a living. Who could tell? Maybe some of them would find their way into the kingdom of heaven without further help from him. Maybe they would even be able to help others find the way—without performing miraculous healing, without casting screaming demons out of demented minds.

When it became obvious that he was going to go without breakfast if he didn't claim his share soon, he got up from his seat on the rock. His first thought was to reach out and grab a loaf as it sailed by, but, this strategy failing because he was unwilling to get too close to the flailing bodies, he edged his way out of the line of fire and managed to pick up one of the last remaining loaves and some fish for himself from Mary's basket. By the time he'd returned to his place on the rock, the bread had stopped flying and the two women were holding their hands in the air to indicate that there was nothing more to throw.

"Did you save something for yourselves?" Jesus called to them.

"We know how to take care of ourselves," Mary called back as she and Perpetua got to their feet and began distributing sardines even though the men were showing absolutely no interest in settling down. Finally, Perpetua gave up any pretense of an equitable sharing of the food and plopped herself in Simon's lap, happily allowing her basket to be ripped out of her grasp. Mary hung on to her own basket, looked toward Jesus, and managed to work her way clear of the commotion, walking to him and beginning to lower herself to the ground next to him.

Jesus leaned over and placed his hand on her arm. "Ants down there," he warned. "They'll be demanding their fair share."

She straightened up, smiled at him, looked down at the ants briefly, and sat down next to him on the rock.

6

The cross is lifted into place and Jesus' weight sags. Instinctively he uses his arms to hold his body in place to relieve the searing agony as these spikes tear through the nerves of his wrists and heels. In the woozy reality that is now his consciousness, he knows that the reflex action of the muscles in his arms will be unable to sustain any lifting action, yet still he lifts against the relentless pull of the earth.

He opens his eyes, staring vaguely through a stinging blur at the desolate hills that rise to the west. To his left he hears the laughter of the guards as they move away in the direction of Herod's palace. Unable to turn his head, he listens with an excruciating intensity that magnifies the voices even as they fade and die.

Today felt especially good. Trudging about through Galilee had become a daily routine for Jesus, often with Mary Magdalene at his side. Sometimes their day was filled with crowds of people seeking a cure for endless maladies. Sometimes they encountered hostile village leaders and accusations of satanic empowerment. Sometimes they sat quietly with one or two who shared a humble meal in return for the hope that Jesus offered. This warm summer sabbath morning felt different.

The eight mile hike northward from Magdala to Hazor was not particularly difficult, but the group moved slowly. There was no urgency in this trek. Except for Phillip, whose pace kept him always out in front, hurrying ahead and then waiting impatiently for the others to catch up, they moved with a sense of camaraderie rather than purpose. After all, there was little at Hazor except ancient ruins and a scattering of small houses. In its day, hundreds of years earlier, Hazor had been a large, fortified city, but now tenant farmers struggled to survive. Elaborately engineered walls and water systems were buried deep beneath accumulated layers of earth.

Tomorrow the two of them would turn northwest toward the port city of Tyre. Today, however, would be spent relaxing with a few of the growing number of disciples who had declared themselves willing to devote their lives to helping others by spreading the truth of the kingdom of heaven. They trailed at the rear of this group of 16, stopping to investigate every interesting sign of life along the road: flowered plants, newly dug animal burrows, basking lizards, tracks in the soft earth. Many small streams meandered through the area, eventually finding their way to join the flow of the Jordan into the Sea of Galilee. These kept the vegetation fresh and green almost year-round. In the distance, set in a rising panorama of green fields and cloud-streaked blue sky, Mount Hermon rose heavenward.

Beyond them, as they watched in amusement, John mischievously pulled a clump of sod from the side of the road and hurled it indiscriminately in the direction of those who were walking ahead. The missile struck the unsuspecting Simon on the back of the head, bursting into hundreds of dirt particles that disintegrated in his hair and rained downward against his neck and inside his tunic. The fisherman let out a shout of surprise, leaned over and shook his head to rid himself of the dirt, and then gyrated in a frantic dance of discomfort, pulling his tunic up over his head and brushing violently at it and his shoulders. Eventually, his tunic back in place, he turned to identify his attacker from among the laughing companions. Everyone, of course, by word and gesture, proclaimed his innocence.

"Teacher!" Simon roared when it became clear that his friends were not going to help. "You saw who did it. Point to the guilty man. An eye for an eye! It's my just due."

Jesus smiled and raised his hands, palms up, to indicate his inability to help.

"Teacher!" Simon pleaded.

"Turn the other cheek," Phillip called to him, evoking a series of boisterous suggestions from several others: "Let him have your coat." "Go an extra mile." "Give him your money."

Simon turned his head to look at each man who called out, pausing and seeming to consider each suggestion. Then, after shaking his head again and using his hands to rough up his hair, he grinned. "That's exactly what I want to do," he said, adopting a conciliatory tone, "but how can I give him my coat if I don't know who he is?"

"It was John!" Mary shouted.

Jesus immediately turned and placed himself so that he faced Mary with his back to Simon and the group. He raised his arms skyward. "Come out of this woman, you unclean spirit!" he commanded.

For a brief moment, everyone was quiet.

"It was John!" Mary shouted again, even louder than before, peering around Jesus and pointing in accusation at the son of Zebedee, who still stood off the road in grass that reached to his knees.

With an explosion of air like a cough and sneeze combined, Jesus released the laugh he'd been choking inside. Mary's husky, rolling guffaw exploded in response. She fell against him and let him wrap his arms around her and support her and laugh deliciously, silently, with her. His shoulders shook, his chest heaved, his eyes watered.

The moment—the lifetime—enveloped Jesus like a joyous vacuum, releasing every pain, transforming every sorrow, nourishing every hunger. He gave in to it, basking in the freedom of it until, reluctantly, he had to let the sweet laughter wane, settle into a soft glow, and, finally, subside. He was aware of the warmth of the sun on his back and the living warmth of the woman Mary in his arms. He gave her an extra squeeze, rejoiced in a squeeze of response from her arms around his waist, and let his own arms drop.

Summoning as much solemnity as his still laughing mind would allow, Jesus turned, grasped his hands behind his back, and addressed the issue of Simon's request.

He felt Mary's hands wrap themselves around his.

"Mary believes that John is the man to whom you should give your coat," he announced with what he intended to be authority.

Simon nodded his thank you, turned to scrutinize John, and took a few steps in that direction.

John smiled uncertainly.

Simon smiled in return. "I'll give him a coat," he promised.

John broke and ran toward Mount Hermon, bounding like a frightened deer over the long grass. Simon was immediately at his heels, powering through the undergrowth in pursuit. Behind them on the road, the disciples hooted and hollered in support of one man or the other even though it must have been clear to everyone that escape was impossible. Simon, gaining with every long stride, was soon able to reach out and, with both hands on John's shoulders, drive his prey to the earth.

Immediately the shouting ceased as each onlooker gazed in silence at the spot where the two men had tumbled. For an instant, neither man could be seen, but almost immediately Simon's head and shoulders appeared amid a flurry of dirt and grass that rose like a cloud above the two. And then, abruptly, it was over. The big man stood up, stared down at the still out-of-sight John, and then began striding back toward the group. He had almost reached the road when John stood up, brushing and shaking and spitting.

Simon stopped and twisted his body to watch as John, still struggling to rid himself of the coat of dirt, begin his own trek back. He watched motionless until John had almost reached the road. Then Simon turned to grin at Jesus, whooping loudly and raising both huge arms in victory. "I *love* that man!" he roared.

7

A nauseating vision of the two crosses to his right undulates in his consciousness. His nasal passages are crusted with blood and mucus. The area between his eyes throbs as though the full weight of a man in an iron boot were pressing against his face. Still, the putrid odor of decay from the rotting flesh of the corpses that still dangle next to him persists in all its odious intensity.

A pulsating silence engulfs him.

In the only direction that his position allows him to view, a solitary figure, real enough despite the diffusing haze that is his mind, waits in the morning gloom. He is not alone. Jesus closes his eyes, not needing them to retain the image of that figure, not needing them to hold on to the presence that will sustain him. Death would come when it would come—in minutes, hours, days. He would not be alone when it came.

In the shade beneath a cedar, in what probably was once the location of the city of Hazor, Jesus sat himself on the trunk of a fallen tree at the side of the road and motioned for the others to sit as well. He watched in amusement as Simon flopped on the thick layer of pine needles and stretched himself out full length, back to the ground, eyes to the branches overhead and the blue sky beyond. John, not surprisingly, lay down next to him, his arms spread out so that his right arm rested across Simon's Adam's apple. Simon wordlessly lifted the arm and placed it behind his head so that he could use it as a pillow. The group had been together long enough now so that Jesus could anticipate how each would place himself. Except for Mary, who sat with her back to the tree trunk at Jesus' feet, the women would sit outside the circle at the rear of the group. Andrew would settle, legs crossed, directly in front of him. Philip and Nathanael would remain standing, Philip pacing restlessly behind the group and Nathanael set rigidly, his arms folded across his chest to Jesus' left.

"I'm hungry," Simon grumbled to no one in particular.

Jesus watched in silence as Perpetua uncovered the basket of bread and fish she'd been carrying, waving her off as she got to her knees and held the basket in his direction. "Feed my sheep," he said, wondering as he spoke the words just where they had come from. First of all, he was hungry. By the time this mob had taken as much as they wanted, there might well be nothing left for him. Second, sheep weren't especially smart animals. Referring to these disciples as sheep could hardly be taken as a compliment. An apology rested on the tip of his tongue, but he decided to swallow it. No one seemed to have heard, and, more interestingly, a little play was unfolding as Perpetua purposely avoided Simon, even having to step over his prone body as she distributed the food. Simon, who sat up as his wife moved away from him, also watched as each disciple reached into the basket for his share.

"So, what about him?" Simon asked with a nod of the head toward John when everyone but the two of them had been fed. John was still stretched out on his back, his eyes closed. "I don't mind doing without,"

Simon added with feigned magnanimity. "Feed my sheep." He looked at Jesus and grinned.

John's eyes popped open and followed Perpetua as she again bypassed Simon and stopped next to him. Sitting up as though it were a considerable effort, he reached into the basket, running his hand around the inside in an imagined search. "Ah," he said finally, looking at Simon as he pulled out a small chunk of bread. "I think I got the last piece." He held it in Simon's direction. "Here, you deserve it more than I," he said with exaggerated compassion.

Simon grabbed the bread and stuffed it into his mouth with one bite. "You're right," he said as he chewed.

Nathanael stood watching, still maintaining an apparent aloofness yet quietly involved in the horseplay of his friends. It was Nathanael's eyes, Jesus decided, that made people uncomfortable: brooding, penetrating eyes beneath heavy brows.

Possibly Nathanael felt Jesus' gaze. The eyes narrowed and veiled themselves as they connected with Jesus. "Teacher," he called, "can we get down to business?"

Jesus looked at him and smiled tentatively. Getting down to business was necessary, to be sure, but always there was plenty of business. How often did they have the opportunity to enjoy a good laugh?

Nathanael's scowl deepened, magnified somehow by a dark, uneven growth of facial hair. Nathanael's face always looked just like that. Never a beard. Always a few days' growth. How odd! How odd that he would notice! How odd that the realization seemed significant!

"Nathanael is correct," Jesus said. "It's time to settle down." He scanned the faces of the men and women around him. "First, though," he added, directing his attention to Perpetua, "is there anything left in that basket?"

8

His arms fatigue. Cramps sweep through his muscles, knotting them in disabling pain, making it almost impossible to pull himself upward to breathe. His body slips downward, reminding him anew of the bloody, lacerated tissue on his back as it is pressed against the rough surface of the wood. A terrible, constricting cramp builds in his chest as his lungs cry out for air. His legs stiffen against the nails. His shoulders and arms fight against the cramps to pull himself upward and allow his lungs to exhale and to suck new, life sustaining air past his swollen, cracked lips.

"Teacher," Philip was saying, "we've got to get organized."

Jesus nodded, wanting Philip to know that his input was appreciated but not wanting to give the people of Galilee the impression that a legion of disciplined disciples was marching forth to tell people how to live their lives. "What do you have in mind?" he asked.

Philip wiped the top of his bald head with one hand and stared down at the ground for a few seconds. "Well," he said, looking up at Jesus, "We should have some basic procedure to follow."

"Such as?"

"For one thing, we shouldn't carry any money."

"What's the point in that?" James interrupted, looking at Jesus rather than turning to address Philip.

Jesus raised his hand. "Let him finish," he said, pleasantly aware of Mary's hand resting on his foot.

"Don't wear sandals," Philip continued. "Extend the peace greeting to each house and accept whatever hospitality is offered. Eat what is set before you."

James broke in again. "Suppose an animal hasn't been slaughtered properly. Suppose there's still blood in the meat!"

"Or catfish," John chimed in. "Suppose they plop a catfish on our plate."

"That's not going to happen," Philip argued.

"Of course it's going to happen," Jesus insisted, immediately commanding everyone's attention even though he had not raised his voice. "You're talking about sitting down to eat with poor people. These folks can't concern themselves with the niceties of the dietary laws. They're worried about survival."

"Teacher," Simon moaned, "I can't face a filthy catfish on my plate, even if I'm starving."

"Have you ever been starving?" Jesus asked.

"He's always starving," John laughed.

"No," Simon admitted, ignoring John's barb. "I've never been starving."

"A nice juicy rabbit roasted over a spit would probably taste mighty fine to a starving man," Jesus suggested.

Simon stared at the pine needles covering the ground beneath him, apparently considering Jesus' rabbit. Finally he raised his head and smiled sadly. "God didn't make the laws for no reason," he said. "Clean or unclean. We get to make the choice."

Simon's words hung in the resinous shade beneath the cedar. Jesus gazed into the sunshine beyond, watching two distant figures at work among seemingly endless rows of grape vines that stretched across the rising landscape. His left hand rested on the back of Mary's neck, his fingers, independent of any conscious intent, gently massaging, kneading, responding to the warmth of her being.

"*After all,*" he said at last, speaking not only to Simon but to John and Nathanael and Philip...to everyone there beside the road...perhaps mostly, speaking to himself, "*what goes into your mouth will not defile you.*" He paused, now focusing on only Simon. "*It's what comes out of your mouth that will defile you,*" he added.

Nathanael's deep voice rumbled to Jesus' left. "We can eat anything we want then."

Jesus turned his head to acknowledge the statement but said nothing.

"Is that right?" Nathanael persisted.

"You can eat anything you want," Jesus answered, "with anybody you want." He resisted the urge to amplify the statements. These men and women should have accepted by now the truth that all human beings are equal in the eyes of God. How often had he and they already been accused of sitting down to eat with tax collectors, sinners, and whores? How often had he been called a glutton and a drunkard? It wasn't such a big step from gluttony to impurity. In the eyes of those who see themselves as superior to others, there would be no difference at all.

He decided to change the subject. "Is that it then, Philip?" he asked. "Any more rules?"

Philip, his face glistening with sweat, stopped his pacing and turned to face Jesus. "The rules aren't the point," he said.

Jesus raised his eyebrows but said nothing. Perhaps this discussion was going to take on some substance after all.

"The point," Philip continued, "is attitude. It's all about who we are, about how we present ourselves to the people we meet. No one's going to listen if we just walk into their homes and tell them how they should live their lives. If we have money and clean clothes and wear sandals, they'll see us just as they see the Sadducees and Romans and publicans and land owners."

"So we should look like we're poor," Simon summarized. "That shouldn't be difficult."

Next to him, John stood up, holding his arms away from his sides, palms up, and slowly turning in a circle to display himself to everyone there. "Behold," he announced. "Poverty. Honesty. Divinity."

"Sandals," Nathanael protested. "The sandals give you away."

"He's a Sadducee in disguise," James added.

John looked from Nathanael to James and then down at his feet, seeming to study them intently for several seconds before raising his head and speaking in the direction of Philip. "I'm not giving up my sandals," he said. "Rules or no rules."

"Wear your damn sandals," Philip answered, obviously exasperated.

"I'm not walking these roads barefoot," John grumbled as he sat down, winking to Simon as he settled himself on the pine needles.

Jesus waited for the wisecracks to subside before continuing. "There's no virtue in being poor," he began. "How is it different? Taking pride in being rich and powerful, or taking pride in being poor and independent?"

He paused to let his words sink in. What point was he trying to make? Cynics had been wandering the land for 400 years, seeking happiness through freedom, refusing to accept society's material values, scoffing at the customs and conventionalities of others. Would it serve any purpose to talk about the Cynics to these men and women, to try to illustrate how the very pursuit of freedom must inevitably result in subjugating yourself to a set of rules?

Nathanael's deep rumble broke into Jesus' thoughts. "But you said…"

Jesus finished the sentence for him. "The poor are to be congratulated."

Their eyes met.

Jesus motioned for him to come into the circle, indicating a spot directly in front of himself where Nathanael could sit. After a brief hesitation, the young man moved to the spot and lowered his body until he sat cross-legged on the pine needles facing Mary Magdalene.

"The poor are to be congratulated," Jesus began hesitantly, "not because they are poor and weak but because the kingdom of heaven is more readily available to them than it is to the rich and powerful." He searched Nathanael's eyes but could not penetrate their defenses.

"Teacher…" Simon began.

Anticipating the question, Jesus held up his hand. He needed a story. "*Someone was giving a big dinner and invited many guests,*" he began. "*At the dinner hour, the host sent his slave to tell the guests, 'Come, it's ready; now.' But one by one they all began to make excuses. The first said to him, 'I just bought a farm, and I have to go and inspect it; please excuse me.' And another said, 'I just bought five pairs of oxen, and I'm on my way to check them out; please excuse me.' And another said, 'I just got married, and so I cannot attend.' So the slave came back and reported these excuses to his master. Then the master of the house got angry and instructed his slave: 'Quick! Go out into the streets and alleys of the town, and usher in the poor, and crippled, the blind, and the lame.'*"

Even in the shade of the cedar, the heat of the day seemed to Jesus to be enveloping the group of disciples. For a while, there was no response at all to his story. Lethargy sat on them like a fat hen on a nest full of eggs.

Nathanael broke the spell. "The poor and crippled did nothing to deserve their invitation," he said, almost to himself.

"As far as we know," Jesus pointed out, excited to have heard from this reluctant disciple, "none of the guests, rich or poor, had done anything to deserve the invitation."

Nathanael raised his head to look at Jesus, a trace of a smile in his eyes but not on his lips. "You don't have to earn your way into the kingdom of heaven," he said.

Jesus waited for him to continue, to carry the idea to its conclusion.

The set of Nathanael's jaw relaxed ever so slightly. "The poor were available," he added.

"And hungry," Mary suggested. She twisted her head to look up at Jesus.

He squeezed her shoulder.

Nathanael wasn't yet ready to let go of the analogy. "But, at first, why did the man invite only his wealthy friends? Why didn't he invite everyone?"

From the rear of the group, Philip interrupted. "We're not talking soup kitchen, here," he called out impatiently. "Obviously, there wasn't room at the table for everyone."

Nathanael twisted his body to look at Philip and then turned to question Jesus with his eyes.

It was a good question. Why hadn't the man told his slave to invite everyone? There were no seating limitations in the kingdom of heaven. He smiled at Nathanael. "I'll tell the story that way next time," he said.

9

A low, agonizing moan rumbles involuntarily deep in his chest. He would suppress it but cannot. It is not so much from him as of him. He has no more control of it than of the sun passing beyond the mournful sky of this day that is both beginning and end.

Beginning and end.

Twist. Pull with shoulder muscles seared by pain. Push against the torn nerves in his heels.

Cough to expel the foulness from his lungs.

Gasp for air.

Edge downward against the rough grain of the wood, against the agonizing pain in his heels and his wrists as they accept their share of the weight of his exhausted body.

"Do you really think that's the way it works?" Mary asked.

Jesus answered without looking at her, distracted by the stretch of sandy beach between the two of them and the harbor of Tyre beyond.

"I think so," he said. "Trying to explain God is futile. The fact is, if we could explain him, he wouldn't be God."

On the shore directly ahead of where the two of them were standing, a boat about the size of those in Zebedee's fleet had been beached, its stern rising and falling as sets of gentle waves moved across the sand beneath it.

"But you told Nathanael that he could heal people."

Jesus nodded. A solitary figure was sitting on the gunwale of the boat, his legs dangling over the side.

"You said anybody can be a healer."

He placed his hand on her arm and nudged her toward the boat.

Mary didn't move. "You're ignoring me," she said. "I hate when you do that."

He grinned and leaned to kiss her on the cheek.

She turned her head. "Now you're being condescending."

"I'm not being condescending," he protested. "Yes, anyone can be a healer. Why is that a problem?"

She turned to face him. "It's not a problem," she said. "It just doesn't seem like it could be true. I've never healed anybody."

"How do you know?" His discussion with Nathanael was replaying in his mind now—the frustration, the sense of inadequacy, sweeping through him just as it had at the time. The power of God…the force of God…the love of God was all around them, all the time, he'd promised. Healing the sick was nothing more than putting that power to work, of bringing the force—the love—through oneself and directing it into the person who needed healing.

"I know because no sick person has ever walked away healthy after I've done the magic hands-on routine."

"But who's to say that none of them ever felt better when they got home?" he suggested. "Who's to say that none of them woke up the next morning and put in a good day's work in the field?"

"They didn't," she insisted. "I know they didn't."

He chose not to press the point. She was probably right. And probably for the same reason that all the disciples had failed.

"I didn't have faith," she said, her voice so faint that Jesus could barely hear the words. "I don't have faith," she added.

He thought of the man sitting on the boat and looked over his shoulder to see if he was still there. Nothing had changed. The man sat on the gunwale, the waves lapped against the sandy beach, and other, larger ships rode peacefully at anchor in the harbor. He returned his attention to Mary. "You know what I told Nathanael and the others," he said.

She nodded. "It's a frame of mind." There was a long pause. "They have to connect with God."

"Yes."

"They have to enter the kingdom of heaven."

"Yes." A cool, onshore breeze blew a strand of hair down in front of his eyes, and he pushed it back. "I didn't think I could do it either," he said, "not in the beginning." And what had changed his mind? What had happened to his doubt? Where had it gone? If he could pinpoint the moment, the event, he'd then be able to answer Mary's and Nathanael's questions with some useful advice, with something more than vague reassurances.

They were walking now. The sand gave way under his sandal with each step, getting under the straps and grating uncomfortably against his top of his feet.

"Why wouldn't healing be like everything else?" Mary asked.

"Like everything else what?"

She stopped, allowing him to plod on for a few more steps before turning to look back at her. "Like singing," she suggested, looking past him toward the harbor. "Not everybody can carry a tune. Like dancing or working with numbers or..."

"Or catching a fish," he offered.

She studied his face, apparently trying to decide if he was taking her seriously. "Yes," she answered. "Like catching a fish. Some people are good at it and some aren't." She took the few steps necessary to move next to him, where she stopped and looked up at him, the question still written on her face.

Maybe she was right. Maybe it was unrealistic to expect the disciples to be healers—some of them, maybe, but not all. "Maybe," he said.

Mary bent down, using one hand to hold onto Jesus and balance herself while she lifted her foot, untied her sandal, and removed it. "Sand's hot," she said after setting the bare foot down and switching hands to remove the other sandal.

"That's a surprise," Jesus said.

"You should take yours off, too," Mary said as she straightened up, both sandals dangling from one hand.

Jesus didn't answer, instead turning and striding, purposefully now, toward the water with Mary hurrying to keep up. Inexplicably, it seemed important that he speak with the man on the boat. This was not about healing. It was not about sharing the word of God. There was a significance about this man that Jesus could not identify, a sense of urgency that he could not explain.

The sand was damp and tightly packed as they neared the water. To their right, perhaps 20 paces away, the man watched like a giant housefly, eyes bulging in the glare of the mid-day sun. Oddly ill at ease under this scrutiny, Jesus watched over his shoulder as Mary caught up with him. She hesitated when she got to his side but then proceeded, her steps slow and cautious, past him and into the forward edge of the water as it washed over her feet. When the retreating water rippled past her, she looked down at her toes and wiggled them into the wet sand. The next wave, slightly more aggressive, covered her ankles as it slipped past. She turned and grinned. "Oh, God," she said, her voice husky with passion, "you've got to try this." She hiked her tunic up to her knees and waded further into the surf.

It was too tempting to resist. Jesus sat down and began unlacing his sandals, immediately regretting his choice as the wet sand soaked the back of his tunic. But it was too late to do anything about that. It would probably be a lot wetter soon. When his sandals were off, he stood up and tossed them and his knapsack behind him onto the dry sand. "Give me yours," he shouted, wading out to where Mary stood, tunic in one hand, sandals in the other. He took the sandals from her, splashed back to the water's edge, tossed them near his own, and then turned to watch Mary, who had waded out even further and was now jumping as each small wave swept past, each time raising the water level above her knees.

The cool water felt wonderful against his scorched, bruised feet.

Mary, laughing, turned and called to him. "Come out deeper. You'll love it."

He was tempted, but somehow it didn't seem respectable to lift his tunic as Mary was doing, not with Fly Eyes watching in disapproval nearby. But that wasn't fair. The man might be laughing and enjoying their enthusiasm as much as they. Why had he already labeled the man as stiff necked and critical?

"Come on!" Mary called again.

He responded impulsively, breaking into a high-stepping, bouncing run toward her and past her until the water was too deep to continue and then diving head first into the next approaching wave.

10

Love your enemies.

Within the sticky, overheated fog that is his mind, Jesus tries unsuccessfully to focus on that thought. Love your enemies. This is at the heart of the kingdom, he is certain, yet it is the reason that his nude, bloody, pathetic body is pinned, writhing in agony, to a tree of shame.

Saul's eyes continued to fascinate Jesus as he and Mary sat with the man on the sand next to the boat. Comparing them to the bulging eyes of a fly had been unkind and not really accurate. It wasn't so much that they bulged. They were very large and deep green and intense, but that wasn't it either. Somehow, beneath heavy brows and receding hairline, set narrowly against an aquiline nose, the eyes, like those of an eagle, intimidated, analyzed, demanded your attention. An eagle! That was it. Saul of Tarsus was an eagle, not a housefly.

Behind Saul, draped over the side of the boat, Jesus' wet tunic was a continuing reminder of the price, and the joy, of spontaneity. Fortunately, Philip's suggested rule of not carrying spare clothing had not been well received by the disciples. After all, as Andrew had pointed out, a knapsack, sandals, and a staff were not exactly symbols of wealth. Who, in fact, would want to listen to the ravings of a stranger who didn't have enough sense to protect himself from the elements? Andrew didn't talk much, but he listened, and pondered, and, when he did speak, got to the essence of a matter quickly and easily.

Saul was a tent maker, he'd told them in a long biographical account that seemed more like a speech than a friendly conversation struck up casually on the beach. It was a family business. He was Jewish but a citizen of Rome, his grandfather having purchased citizenship for 500 drachmae many years before. The Roman army needed huge leather tents for the legions, using the expensive gear for their winter quarters. Each tent housed eight men and was ten Roman square feet in size.

"So you tan leather," Mary asked.

Saul's eyes scornfully examined Mary's face before responding. "No," he said.

Mary glanced quickly at Jesus as though seeking permission to continue and then went on without any response from him, which was precisely what he wanted her to do. In the first place, she didn't need his permission, and, in the second place, she was going exactly where he might have gone had she not beaten him to it. "But tents are made with tanned leather," she persisted. "You have to kill a cow or a goat or a pig..."

"No pigs," Saul interrupted quietly.

"You have to skin the animal..."

Saul's large lips were set in a condescending smile, his head nodding slowly in response to Mary's words.

"There's a lot of blood."

More mistrustful nods.

"And the bloody hide has to be scraped with a dull knife and pounded to remove any pieces of meat and fat."

Saul shifted his eyes to Jesus, almost smiling. "She's good," the eyes said.

"The hair on the outer part of the skin..."

"Yes! Yes!" Saul interrupted. "It's a rotten business. What's your point?"

"Tanning leather is forbidden," Jesus said, suddenly impatient to get to the question that, like a bow drawn taut as a leery beast approaches, silently awaited the moment of the kill. "Mary is wondering..."

"I don't tan leather," Saul repeated. "The world is full of non-Jews whose Gods don't care one way or the other about blood and decay. In Tarsus many people worship Mithras." His voice was getting louder now. "They drink the blood of the sacred bull as it is ritually slain. They bathe in the blood. They rub it into their eyes, ears, nostrils. The blood symbolizes the transfer of life and power. Do you think such people are going to be squeamish about tanning leather?"

"Mary is wondering, I think," Jesus continued, "if perhaps you, a devout Jew, become unclean by employing such people." There it was. The arrow had been launched.

Saul silently assessed Mary out of the corner of his eagle eyes, seeming to consider whether this subject and these two wanderers were worth the expenditure of his time and the application of his intellect. It was Jesus' guess that he would decide that they were not. Probably Saul would leave them and return to his perch on the gunwale of the boat. That expectation brought up another intriguing question: how would this wealthy, intellectual tanner of hides manage to get back aboard without seeming to be in retreat? Saul of Tarsus was not a big man. How would he scramble back aboard without presenting the image of a timid animal seeking refuge in a tree?

Saul got slowly to his feet. Instead of returning to the boat, he began pacing in a sort of limping gate, as though one leg were shorter than the other, around the spot where Jesus and Mary sat. "I am an educated man," he began. "For you, I speak Aramaic, but Greek is my first language. I think in Greek. I write in Greek. Still, I am a Jew. I have undergone a thorough training in the Pharisaic schools. In regard to the Law, I am a Pharisee." He stopped his pacing and stared down at Mary, leaving unsaid what was clearly the heart of his message: he was much more qualified to determine the state of his purity than were a couple of ragamuffins from Galilee who knew no more about God than they did about respectful behavior.

"These men who tan the hides and make the tents..." he continued, inserting a pause that felt affected and patronizing, "...these men work because they choose to. I pay them well. If they didn't tan hides for me, they would tan them for someone else. It's not my responsibility to enforce the Law. The Lord has given us the conditions of our covenant with him. I keep that covenant. Others do not." He continued his pacing, his left shoulder dropping and rising with each step. "So much for them," he added, almost to himself.

Mary, was sitting cross-legged, learning forward, watching her finger trace over and over a design in the sand, perhaps waiting for Saul to continue his lecture, perhaps lost in thought about some subject entirely unrelated to the physical moment.

Saul paced silently—up, down, up, down—completing several circuits.

Jesus studied Mary's face, knowing that she was not finished with the little eagle, knowing that, the arrow having been launched with precision, she would not fail to make certain of the kill.

"Saul of Tarsus," she said without looking up from her design, "you speak of the cult of Mithras. You speak of many gods."

"There is only one God!" Still he circled.

"And that one God. Does he care only for Jews?"

Saul stopped. "The One God has given us the Law," he answered, looking not at Mary but at the horizon beyond the ships at anchor. "The Law does not discriminate."

"But it was given to Moses, to the Israelites...the Chosen People."

"Aha," Saul replied, pointing a finger triumphantly at Mary. "The One God chose to *give* the Law to the Jews, but it is not for only them."

Mary stopped tracing the design in the sand and looked up at Saul. "Then Mithras worshippers can love God just as you do," she said. "Greeks and Romans can love God just as you do."

Dramatically Saul moved to sit down next to Mary. "The fact, dear lady," he began, "the fact is that I do *not* love God. Greeks and Romans do not love God. You..." he pointed at her again, "...do not love God. Your friend here..." He motioned with an open hand toward Jesus. "...does not love God." He waited, seeming to savor the shock value of what he had just said.

"My friend," Jesus said quietly, "do not presume to speak for me. Loving God is what my life is about. Loving..."

Saul tried to interrupt, but Jesus held up one hand to silence him.

"Loving God is the sole purpose of every human being's life. '*You are to love the Lord your God with all your heart, with all your soul, with all your energy, and with all your mind*'. You speak of your respect of the Law and yet you disclaim the most important commandment of them all?"

Paul's lips were set in a tight smile as Jesus spoke. Now his eyes widened, illuminated by what might have been a sense of impending victory. "Young man," he began, "you're too quick to take offense. I do not dispute the words of the Law, only its intent. God's love for mankind is certain. God's love is pure and eternal and incredibly beyond the scope of mankind's ability to love in return. God exists to love. He does not need to *be* loved. He needs to be obeyed!"

"Obeyed," Jesus repeated.

"Exactly. Human beings cannot love as God loves. We can like God. We can worship God. We can fear God. But Love? Alas, we are puny, pathetic, fickle creatures. Read the Scriptures. The story of mankind is a shameful one. The more God loves us, the worse we behave."

It was Jesus' turn to stand. He looked down at Mary and smiled, brushed the sand from the back of his tunic, and walked to his wet tunic hanging on the boat, pointlessly feeling of it to see if it had dried. Could Saul be correct? Certainly man's relationship with God had been stormy. How many times had the Lord threatened to destroy his people? How many floods? How many plagues? How many hardships had God inflicted upon his ungrateful, rebellious people? Was this because they were incapable of love? He didn't think so. He and Saul were not talking about the same thing.

He walked back to where Saul and Mary sat watching him and squatted next to the tanner of hides. "*There was a man going from Jerusalem down to Jericho,*" he began, staring at the sand as he spoke, "*when he fell into the hands of robbers. They stripped him, beat him up, and went off, leaving him half dead. Now by coincidence, a priest was going down that road; when he caught sight of him, he went out of his way to avoid him. In the same way, when a Levite came to the place, he took one look at him and crossed the road to avoid him. But this Samaritan, who was traveling that way, came to where he was and was moved to pity at the sight of him. He went up to him and bandaged his wounds, pouring olive oil and wine on them. He hoisted him onto his own animal, brought him to an inn, and looked after him. The next day he took out two silver coins, which he gave to the innkeeper, and said, 'Look after him, and on my way back I'll reimburse you for any extra expense you have had.'*"

A ponderous silence greeted the end of the story. The rhythmic splash of the waves softly broke into Jesus' consciousness, causing him to look up and gaze into the glare of the sun off the water. What was Saul thinking, he wondered? About love? About the price of tanned leather? About where he was going to eat that evening?

"And the point is?" Saul asked at last.

"Human beings love by having compassion for other human beings," Jesus said. "They love God by loving their neighbor."

"By loving their enemy," Mary broke in.

"Yes, by loving their enemy," he repeated reluctantly, having intended to leave that part out. A quick shift of the eyes toward Mary asked her to leave this moment to him. It was doubtful that Saul was ready to cope with loving one's enemies.

"Their enemy," Saul echoed tonelessly.

"Forget that part for now," Jesus instructed. The distinction between God's love of man and man's love of God was an elusive one. How could he make it clear that the two were totally different and yet exactly the same?

"Compassion is love." The words hung in the afternoon sun—out of place—an anomaly like Jesus' soggy tunic.

"Compassion is man's ultimate expression of love."

Saul grunted his skepticism.

"This is not about sympathy," Jesus continued. "Both the priest and the Levite probably felt sorry for the injured traveler. Each had practical reasons for not getting involved, but they might very well have had pangs of conscience as they witnessed the victim, considered his plight, but crossed the road to avoid him. They were sorry for the man but driven by overriding considerations that made stopping to help out of the question."

"Compassion..." Mary's attempt to contribute to the discussion was cut short by another flick of the eyes.

"The Samaritan..." Jesus began.

"Who was the enemy of the traveler," Mary inserted quickly, her eyes connecting with Jesus in a look that said, "I know; I know, but it's an important point."

Jesus held on to the connection for several seconds, his solemn expression gradually evolving into a smile. She was correct. Samaritans and Judeans had been unfriendly neighbors for hundreds of years. The Samaritan was loving his enemy. It was an important point. "The Samaritan," he continued, "was more than a witness. He was experiencing the physical pain and the fear and the sense of loss just as though he *were* the injured traveler. He became *One* with the victim."

"Compassion," Saul rumbled, his tone suggesting an academic, not a spiritual acknowledgement.

"Love!" Jesus replied. "A meaningful connection with the Lord. A loving response to God's love for mankind."

"The kingdom of heaven," Mary suggested.

"The kingdom of heaven," Jesus repeated, smiling. It wasn't such a complicated concept after all.

Saul appeared to be considering the point, gazing solemnly at a mountain of sand that he was constructing with his bare feet. Finally he stood up, methodically destroyed the mountain he'd built, and gazed upward at Jesus, who had stood up as well.

"I've been hearing stories," he said.

Jesus met his gaze but said nothing.

"In Galilee still another messiah has appeared."

Jesus looked at Mary and raised his eyebrows.

"The man is gathering crowds of people wherever he goes, promising the peasants the usual things—escape from poverty, freedom from Roman domination, eternal peace and happiness. They say he heals lepers, returns sight to the blind, drives demons from the possessed."

Jesus held out his hand to Mary and pulled her to her feet. "Messiahs come and messiahs go," he said. "Nothing ever changes. Always the poor remain poor, the rich remain rich, the powerful few oppress the powerless many."

Saul didn't seem to be listening. "This self-proclaimed messiah makes a travesty of the Law."

"How is that?" Jesus asked. Up to a point, exaggerated accounts of his ministry amused and pleased him. Small groups of dubious listeners became rapturous throngs; quiet relief from pain became miraculous cures. Perhaps, over time, the publicity would feed on itself and enable him and the disciples to bring the good news of the kingdom of heaven to ever increasing numbers of people. At the same time, much harm could be done if people were misled by wild, distorted promises instead of reassured by honest truths. He was not God! He could not walk on water or calm storms. What he *could* do was lead broken, disillusioned human beings into a loving relationship with their Creator.

"Well," Saul was saying in response to Jesus' question, "this messiah claims that human beings—not the Lord, mind you, but human beings—established the sabbath. Sacrilege! Sacrilege!"

Is that what he'd taught? He tried now to recall his words, to examine them, to consider their context. "*The sabbath day was created for Adam and Eve, not Adam and Eve for the sabbath day.*" To Saul such a suggestion was irreverent although Jesus hadn't intended it to be so. A day of rest in honor of the Lord was a nice tradition, but to believe that God cared one way or the other was crazy.

"The man consorts with criminals and whores," Saul continued. "He's a glutton and a drunk, they say."

Mary turned to face him, hands on hips. "You haven't met this…what's his name?"

"Jesus," Paul answered, having to tilt his head back to meet her gaze.

"You haven't met this Jesus."

"No." He glanced at Jesus, his eagle eyes bright, obviously enjoying the confrontation.

"You haven't heard him speak. You haven't ever personally spoken with either him or his friends."

"Obviously not."

Mary dropped her arms to her sides in frustration and turned her head to look at Jesus.

"Have you?" Saul asked, his tone suggesting a conspiracy.

"Have I what?" Mary asked in return.

"Have you heard this Jesus speak?"

She hesitated, glanced at Jesus again, and then faced Saul, folding her arms across her chest. "It happens that I have…both of us have."

Saul grinned. "Of course I knew that," he said. "You're two of his followers. Every word you speak makes that clear." He moved past Mary to stand facing Jesus, staring up intently as though he might be recording the facial features for some future need.

"They say this Jesus of Nazareth is the Son of God," Jesus said, flicking his eyes toward Mary, noting her surprise and wondering, himself, why in the world he'd said such a thing. His sense of the absurd was always getting him into awkward situations. And now there was no escape. Irresistibly he reconnected with the unwavering eagle gaze of the tentmaker. It was to be a stare down: juvenile, ego-driven, alienating. If the world needed proof of his mortality, this moment would settle the question once and for all.

Saul broke first, turning away and limping toward his boat, turning again when he reached it and calling back to Jesus. "That's good," he said. "The Son of God. We'll see how the Son of God looks hanging from a tree."

11

Love. What could the word possibly mean? His efforts to piece together an answer are hopelessly futile. Pain—excruciating, all encompassing pain—overwhelms rational thought. Not only can he not will his mind to embrace this idea, he is unable even to recall what the idea was.

It had been Andrew's idea, Jesus was pretty certain. "In ten days, Sukkot will begin," Andrew had pointed out. He hadn't seemed to be suggesting anything in particular that they should do about it. They'd been talking about the imminent arrival of Yom Kippur. John had kidded Simon about needing more than one day to atone for his sins, particularly the sin of picking on people who were smaller than he.

"First of all," Simon had responded, "I don't pick on you. You're a pest, and pests will drive a man crazy if he doesn't swat them now and then. And second, even if I do pick on you, it's not a sin against God. I wouldn't have to repent anyway."

Probably the discussion would have ended at that point. They'd been sitting around the fire in Simon's courtyard. The nights were getting cold now that summer had ended, and, on this particular evening, everyone had seemed tired. The fishermen would be going out in their boats soon; those who worked in the fields were putting in long days at the harvest. Somehow, all of them were finding opportunities to visit nearby communities to talk about the kingdom of heaven, but mostly those efforts had settled into dispassionate obligations rather than exhilarating adventures. Even Jesus was feeling discouraged. Day after day, he and Mary encountered more opposition than support. Convincing people who had lived their lives in hopelessness that serenity and fulfillment were available even within their subjection was not an easy sell.

It was Nathanael who'd picked up on Andrew's comment about Sukkot. Nathanael was always ready to try anything. Probably he'd never celebrated the Festival of Ingathering in his life. Probably he wasn't even sure what the holiday was all about, so it wasn't that there was any sense of obligation in his suggestion, no thought that celebrating the harvest had anything at all to do with his faith—with God. It was much more likely that Nathanael thought it would be great sport to travel to Jerusalem—preferably by way of Samaria where their presence would be unwelcome—and build themselves a sukkah.

On the other hand, the idea more than likely could be traced back to Mary. More than any of them realized, almost every worthwhile thing the disciples did as a group could be traced back to Mary. While Nathanael was the one who finally generated enthusiasm for the decidedly impractical trek to Jerusalem, it was almost certain that Mary had done some serious sowing of seed before Nathanael commenced the harvest. *The kingdom of heaven was like that. Someone sows seed on the ground. The farmer sleeps and rises night and day. The seed sprouts and matures—how, he himself does not know. The soil produces the crop by itself; first the blade, then the head, then the mature grain in the head. It is only then that the farmer puts in the sickle because it's time for the harvest.*

And so, here they were, skirting Mount Ebal in their approach to Sychar, two days travel from Jerusalem. Nathanael, striding ahead with Philip, seemed tireless, the two of them laughing and joking and laying plans for a grand entrance into the sacred city. The scenario, already impractical as their imaginations fed on each other, was well on its way to being ludicrous. Jesus, straggling at the rear of the strung-out line of two dozen disciples, put two fingers to his mouth and whistled shrilly to get Philip's attention. Ordinarily, stopping at Jacob's well outside of Sychar would have been a given, but who knew what these two guys would do today? Their minds were set on getting to Jerusalem...on organizing a triumphant parade into the city...on building three elaborate sukkahs that the disciples could live in for the seven days of the festival. If Jesus didn't insist that they stop for food and water, Nathanael and Philip might power right on past the well and the town. They'd trudge over instead of around the graying bald pate of Mount Gerizim in the distance. All of them would die of thirst and exhaustion—no grand entrance, no cheering crowds of followers, no sukkahs. Well, okay, like Nathaneal, he was letting his imagination get away from him.

Nathanael stopped and looked back.

"I hate when you do that," Mary complained.

Jesus kept his eye on Nathanael, raising his arm and pointing up the valley between the two weathered mountains. "When I do what?" he asked.

"That whistling thing you do," Mary said. "It shatters me. It splits me right in half. You could at least give me a warning."

Nathanael waved in response and began moving up the barren valley toward Sychar.

Jesus looked at Mary. "I can't give you a warning," he said. "It's not a thing I contemplate and make a decision about. It just happens."

Mary resumed walking. "That's dumb," she said as he caught up to her.

"I'm thirsty," he said. "I was afraid those two would take us right on past the well."

They continued in silence, heading west up the valley slope now, the late afternoon sun in their eyes. Jesus tried not to think about his thirst. That would be taken care of soon enough. More important was what he was actually going to do when they reached Jerusalem. If Saul of Tarsus could be believed, word of Jesus' challenges to the Law had reached far beyond Galilee. Caiaphas and the Sanhedrin already viewed him as a messenger of Satan. Could he—should he—enter the city unobtrusively and celebrate Sukkot anonymously? That's what he would like to do, but these days his life didn't feel like it was his own. It wasn't a matter of what he wanted to do. Yes, he was making his own decisions, directing his steps this way or that according to his own assessment of a situation. He had choices. Yet, at the same time, there was always this central, inner voice guiding him, judging this choice and that choice so that one or the other always felt right. Was this free will? It didn't feel like it. He could be at peace only when he listened to the voice, and the voice invariably led him to the people. Only when his message was one of love, only when he was risking everything to promote the kingdom of heaven could he be certain that he was risking nothing.

"You aren't really going to go along with their crazy plan, are you?" Mary asked.

Up ahead, about a half mile outside of town, Nathanael and Philip had reached the well. They were talking to a woman who apparently had made the walk from town to draw water.

Jesus grinned. "I might," he said. "No one's going to find out about the kingdom of heaven if I sneak into the city and hide under a bunch of tree branches for seven days." He laughed as he envisioned himself entering the city astride a donkey, the most recent twist offered up by the orchestrating duo. "You have to let go of your inhibitions," Philip had enthused two nights earlier as they'd sat close to a flickering fire, attempting to ward off the chill of the autumn air by enthusiastically exercising their imaginations. "Picture yourself riding the ass like a king astride a bejeweled camel as we approach the city walls. Picture the rest of us lining the road, spreading palm branches along the road ahead of you." At that point Nathanael had stood up, waving an imaginary branch over his head. "Hosanna to the Son of David," he shouted. "Blessed is he who comes in the name of the Lord. Hosanna in the highest." He placed the branch on the ground as though he were making way for the king and then stretched both arms toward the star-filled sky, pushing the damp night air through a restriction in the back of his throat in imitation of the roar of a great crowd. It had drawn supporting shouts and laughter from the disciples at the perimeter of the circle. It had been funny, no doubt about it, funny enough at the time to elicit a tight smile from Jesus and a tentative grin from Mary, but now, as they trudged the final 100 yards toward Jacob's well, the idea seemed preposterous. The only plan that made sense was the one that had them gathering branches as they approached the city, quietly constructing a sukkah with two and a half walls and a sparsely covered roof, and using that structure as the control center for a week of teaching throughout Jerusalem.

"The lamp," Mary said.

He looked at her, puzzled. How had a lamp gotten into the conversation?

"You said there was no point in hiding under a bunch of tree branches. It made me think of the lamp."

He nodded, recalling his own words. "*Since when is the lamp brought in to be put under the bushel basket or under the bed? It's put on the lampstand, isn't it?"* It was one thing to have a store of wise sayings available to tell other people how to live their lives. It was quite another to apply the wisdom to your own life.

Simon was holding out a cup of water for him as he approached the well. "This woman is generously sharing her water pot," Simon explained, indicating with a nod of the head the woman Jesus had seen from a distance.

Jesus lifted the cup in the woman's direction to indicate his appreciation before handing the cup to Mary and watching as she held the cup with the fingers of both hands and quietly sipped.

From behind him, the woman's voice cut through the chatter of the disciples. "How is it that you, being a Jew, are willing to accept a drink from me, a Samaritan woman?"

Mary, the cup still at her lips, raised her eyes to Jesus and then shifted her gaze to the woman. Around them, the disciples noisily bantered. Nathanael and Philip sat with their backs against the shady side of the well, silent, seemingly tuned out to the activity around them. "Am I different from you," Mary asked, "because for 700 years we've made no effort to understand one another. Neither of us is a Jew." She sipped again from the cup. "Both of us are Jewish," she added.

Jesus took his own cup from his knapsack, held it out to the woman, and silently watched as she filled it. "Let's turn your question around," he said after drinking deeply. "Why have you, a Samaritan woman, shared your water with a Jew?" He studied her sun-baked eyes as she considered his question. She was not old, he was sure, yet her body slumped with age.

She tiredly shook her head to indicate that she had no answer.

"*Suppose,*" Jesus suggested, "*you have a friend who comes to you in the middle of the night and says to you, 'Friend, lend me three loaves, for a friend of mine on a trip has just shown up, and I have nothing to offer him.' And suppose you reply, 'Stop bothering me. The door is already locked and my children and I are in bed. I can't get up to give you anything'—I tell you, even though you won't get up and give the friend anything out of friendship, yet you will get up and give the other whatever is needed because you'd be ashamed not to.*"

Locked onto his gaze while he told the story, the woman averted her eyes when he'd finished, staring past him toward Mount Gerizim. The Samaritan temple had been built there who knew when? Caananites from times long past had worshipped the Asherim in the high places. As the Jewish people had straggled back to Jerusalem after the exile, many of them married foreign wives and thus were excluded from the reconstructed temple in Jerusalem. Often they had traveled north to Samaria from Judea, taking with them only a modified version of the Torah. Probably this Samaritan woman knew none of the complexities that had shaped her existence until, on this day, she was who she was. She hated Jews. For reasons that she was unlikely to understand, she was to be hated in return.

Mary nudged him with her elbow. "What does the story mean?" she asked in a stage whisper.

He nudged her in return. "Shame and honor," he said without looking at her.

"Shame and honor," she repeated.

He nodded.

Another elbow in his rib cage. "She gave me a cup of water because she'd have been ashamed not to?"

"Hospitality," he said, turning and wrapping his arms about her in a bear hug to avoid still another jab.

"Thanks." The word was muffled by his enclosing arms, and, for a few seconds that might have also been a lifetime, he held her against him. "That makes a lot of sense," she said finally to his chest. "It's shameful not to attend to the needs of a stranger, but it's okay to hate him."

He relaxed his hold on her and kissed her on the forehead. "What can I say?" he asked. "It must be written somewhere."

12

Longing to die, he involuntarily postpones death. The burning muscles in his shoulders respond, not to his will but to the acidic ache in his lungs, lifting, straining, somehow making it possible to expel the poison from his chest. Now his weight again moves him downward within the limits of his splayed, distended arms, and, with hissing inefficiency, he sucks inward the offensive, flesh-polluted air that will prolong his body's struggle to live.

They were almost to Mizpeh, just four miles from Jerusalem, when Jesus made his decision. It wasn't that he'd been worrying over the question continuously for the past two days. The truth was that he hadn't thought about it much at all. There was too much else going on. The group was in high spirits. Their arrival in Jerusalem was about to become a reality instead of a harebrained scheme. The horseplay had intensified, but so had the times of serious examination. Why were they going? What did a festival celebrating the harvest have to do with the kingdom of heaven? What was the City of David going to be like? Many of them had never been out of Galilee.

"Tell us about it, Teacher," Andrew had asked the night before as they lay, not yet ready to sleep, gazing into the star-filled sky near Bethel. "You've been there haven't you?"

"Of course he's been there," Simon growled from the darkness nearby. "So would you have been if you'd listened to me and gone into Jerusalem last spring instead of heading home when we left Bethany beyond the Jordan."

"The Teacher asked us to go back to Galilee with him," Andrew answered. "You're the one who said we'd go."

For some time, there was no response. A profound, penetrating emptiness filled the night. The nocturnal world was out there—hunting, being hunted, surviving, dying.

"Anyway…" Simon's baritone somehow harmonized with the soundless song of the heavens. "…he's been to Jerusalem lots of times. Had to be. You don't get to know what he knows by sitting around in the dirt of Nazareth."

Jesus had let them talk, really only half paying attention, allowing himself, instead, to be immersed in the seemingly endless expanse that was the night sky. Was heaven up there? Where else could it be? On just such a night two thousand years before, perhaps in this very place, Jacob had dreamed of a ladder set on the earth with its top reaching to heaven, with the angels of God ascending and descending. It was the house of God, Jacob had been certain, and he lay at the gate of heaven.

"His parents used to go to Jerusalem every year at the Feast of the Passover," someone was saying, bringing Jesus back to earth. Whose voice was that? Who was it who was taking it upon himself to tell a story that Jesus himself didn't know?

"And how would you know that?" Simon rumbled. "Leave it to the great prophet Philip to know all the answers."

"Am I wrong, Teacher?" Philip questioned. "Haven't you told me that?"

Jesus smiled and reached out in the darkness in search of Mary's hand. Finding it, cold and surprisingly fragile in the chill of the night, he grasped it and allowed her to pull it beneath her blanket and rest it on the pulsating warmth that was her abdomen. "It sounds like a good story, Philip?" he'd spoken into the darkness.

There was a brief silence before Philip spoke again. "And when he's 12, they go up there as always and spend the full number of days. When it's time to leave, they join the caravan and begin the journey back to Nazareth. What they don't know is that Jesus has stayed behind in Jerusalem. They travel for a full day before realizing that the boy isn't with them. Of course they search for him among their relatives and acquaintances before turning around and heading back to Jerusalem."

"So where could this possibly be going?" Simon had interrupted skeptically. "Three days later they find the boy in the temple. He's teaching the teachers."

"Exactly," Philip answered. "He's listening and asking questions that no one has ever asked before. Everyone who hears him is amazed at his understanding. His parents are astonished, but they're also angry. 'Son, why have you treated us this way?' his mother demands. 'Your father and I have been worried sick!' Naturally Jesus looks at them as though they each have two heads. What's the problem, he's wondering? What were they expecting? Didn't they know that he had to be in his Father's house?"

The silence that had descended on the group was profound. Possibly everyone had fallen asleep. Possibly they'd been transported to the temple with Jesus' parents and the teachers and were staring in awe at the 12-year-old who claimed to be the son of God.

Jesus remembered turning onto his side and putting his lips close to Mary's ear. "If they buy that story," he'd whispered, "I have a royal palace in Jerusalem I want to sell them."

Mary turned her head to look at him. "How much do you want for it?" she'd asked.

He'd laughed aloud, more a chuckle than a laugh but unusual enough to catch his attention, to make him aware of it, almost self-conscious about it. Now, thinking back to that laugh under the stars the night before, he was moved by it, transported by it, somehow changed by it. This business of challenging the status quo, of saving people from an ignominious existence, was all too often a solemn, soul draining process. It was Mary who made it tolerable. It was Mary who made it possible for him to stay connected with the humanity of God.

And so they were gathered on the hillside outside the village of Mizpeh, some standing, shading their eyes with their hands as they scanned the landscape to the southeast where the higher elevations of Jerusalem could be discerned in the mid-day sun. Somehow the experience was a disappointment. Shouldn't the great city rise majestically skyward, in its midst, the temple of the Lord ascending highest of all, gold and sparkling and holy? Shouldn't there be a celestial harmony reverberating from on high, even at this distance resonating in their very souls as they gazed in wonder?

"It's brown," Simon muttered, looking over his shoulder at Jesus, perhaps for confirmation.

Jesus kept his eyes on the distant walls. After all, what should they have expected? Unless you're God himself, you build walls out of the material available. It's brownness aside, the very fact that they could see it from this distance was impressive. The plain of Gibeon, actually a series of rolling hills, spread itself below them, its harvested fields almost golden, its groves of fig trees green and laden with purple fruit, date palms and vineyards stretching seemingly to the very gates of the city.

"We're standing on a historical place, Simon," Jesus was moved to point out. "A thousand years ago, before there was a king in Israel, the people used to meet here on this hill in great national emergencies. Many battles were fought on that plain below us."

Simon made a perfunctory, squinting survey before turning and seeking a rock to sit on. Most of the disciples had already done the same, scattering themselves in small groups on the side of the hill, showing little interest in the scenery or in the historical significance of the area. Every hill and valley in Palestine had historical significance. How many battle sites or crumbling buildings do you have to see before it occurs to you that men come and go, fighting their battle for survival and then moving on to wherever men go when they die. How long before you decide that the only battle that matters is the one that each of us is fighting at the moment?

Jesus surveyed the groups until he spotted Nathanael and Philip sitting with James and John in the shade of a huge boulder. The time had come, he reluctantly admitted as he picked his way along the side of the hill toward them, to make some specific plans for the coming days. The men looked up as they saw him approaching and watched silently as he joined them, as he pulled off his headcloth and wiped his face, as he pulled a skin of water from his knapsack and carefully filled his cup.

"So," he began after he'd drunk and wiped his lips with the back of his hand, "where are we going to get a donkey?"

Nathanael grinned, but said nothing.

"Ask—it'll be given to you," Philip answered. *"Seek—you'll find."*

Jesus nodded. *"Knock—it'll be opened for you,"* he said, completing the promise that he shared with them often. They needed a donkey? There would be a donkey. Philip was correct.

The question had been all it took to get Philip started. Already he was pouring forth the plans that he and Nathanael had devised during the past several days. The disciples would go into the city that very afternoon to recruit hundreds of people to line the road and cheer the next day. They would borrow a donkey...

"Borrow?" Jesus interjected.

Philip hesitated but went on without clarifying the term. They would borrow a donkey and bring it back to Jesus, who would be waiting outside the city. Today they would cut branches from trees and stockpile them, distributing them the next morning to the masses of volunteers just before Jesus was placed on the ass.

Jesus held up his hand. "Just one question," he said. "How are you going to get hundreds of people to line the road and wave branches?" He looked from Philip to Nathanael. "Who are these people?" He looked from John to James. "Why in the world are they going to be willing to do this?"

"Ask—it'll…"

"…be given to you." The five of them completed the sentence in unison, finishing with hesitant laughter that managed to disguise the uncertainty that Jesus was sure they were feeling. It wasn't that any of them doubted the Lord's capabilities. What they weren't sure of was what the Lord's point of view would be in regard to their staging a grand procession that would be a show, not an outpouring of genuine passion.

Nathanael was the first to stop laughing. "It's not impossible, you know," he argued. "People know about the Teacher. Not just in Galilee. People know about the healing. They've heard about the kingdom of heaven. I think we can expect to find a lot of people…"

"Hundreds?" Jesus interrupted.

"Thousands!" This time it was John who broke in.

Jesus grinned and playfully tossed his headcloth at John's face. Hundreds! Thousands! It was like the wild story that he'd fed 5,000 people with five loaves and two fish near Bethsaida. Five hundred, maybe. More likely 200. He'd never seen 5,000 people in one place in his life. And as for feeding them…

"You've seen the road, Teacher," Philip pointed out. "People are coming into the city from all over for the festival. There's already a procession. They're in a good mood. They want to celebrate. They'll wave their branches any chance they get. We won't even have to explain what's going on."

"What *is* going on?" Nathanael asked.

Jesus studied the young man's face. Stubbly beard and all, Nathanael was a child, asking innocent questions, accepting extravagant answers, willingly undertaking impossible tasks. "*Let the children come up to me.*" The words formed in Jesus' mind but remained unspoken. "*Don't try to stop them. After all, God's domain is peopled with such as these.*" Children did not need to be introduced to the kingdom of heaven. They came into this world already knowing. It was skepticism and doubt that had to be learned, and, once learned, it was skepticism and doubt that severed the child's oneness with God. Inexplicably, Nathanael's child mind had endured. "What *is* going on?" he had asked. This was not a request for an explanation of the Feast of Tabernacles. It may not have been a question at all. It was an acknowledgement, an intuitive knowing, an indefinable awareness that this festival, this grand entrance, this entire visit to the City of David was part and parcel of the kingdom they sought.

Exasperation and frustration narrowed Philip's eyes and set his mouth in an expression that said more than any words he might have spoken. "We've been over this a hundred times," his eyes said silently. "You can't really want still another explanation," his unmoving lips complained.

"I mean why are we *really* here?" Nathanael asked. "What can we do here that we couldn't do in Galilee? What's all this have to do with the kingdom of heaven?"

Philip shrugged his shoulders and looked to Jesus. All four men were looking at him now. Andrew had joined the group, sitting down next to Nathanael. Jesus sensed several others standing behind him, he in the shade, they in the sun.

What was there to say? He, himself, hardly understood the specifics of their presence in this place. They were here because they were here. Tomorrow would happen as it would happen. Should he try yet again to explain the kingdom of heaven? That, after all, was why they were here. That was always the reason, no matter where they were, no matter what they might be doing.

"*It's like a mustard seed,*" he heard himself say.

There was silence. Even in the shade of the boulder, he felt the enervating effect of the Tishri afternoon.

"*It's the smallest of all seeds,*" he continued, speaking softly, hoping they would see the connection between Nathanael's question and the mustard seed, fearing that they would not. "*But when it falls on prepared soil, it produces a large plant and becomes a shelter for birds of the sky.*" He let his gaze move from face to solemn face, finding no spark of understanding in the eyes, seeing no upturning at the corners of the mouths to suggest a dawning of clarity. It was discouraging. If these men and women didn't understand, how could he hope that others might?

"We are the birds," he continued, still searching the eyes of the others. "The mustard plant is the kingdom of heaven."

Silence. Ordered minds struggling to comprehend apparent disorder.

"But the mustard plant is a weed," Nathanael said, gradually working his way through the cloud of confusion that enveloped them.

Jesus smiled.

"Farmers hate mustard plants. The stuff takes over the fields."

Jesus lowered his chin and stared upward into Nathanael's eyes—waiting—mutely encouraging.

Nathanael grinned and looked from face to face in the group. "The Pharisees, the Sadducees…"

"They're the farmers!" Simon shouted. "They don't want a mustard plant full of birds in their fields!"

Jesus flung his arms into the air. There it was. The kingdom of heaven was like a mustard seed. It felt good watching the others laugh and take credit for figuring it all out. He poured himself another cup of water and basked in the spirited banter around him, remaining silent as the good cheer gradually settled down.

It was Nathanael, of course, who brought the group, now much larger as others on the hill came to find out what the commotion was all about, back to the actuality of the situation. "So," he said, "we're sowing mustard seeds for the next eight days."

"That's what birds do," John laughed.

"That and poop," Simon roared. "We'll spread bird poop all over Jerusalem."

Philip stood up. "This'll be a harvest celebration that no one will soon forget," he said.

Someone began cawing like a crow. Another began to chirp like a sparrow. Almost immediately others picked it up, and the hot afternoon was filled with a cacophony of manmade caws, twitters, warbles, coos, and chirps.

Jesus felt a hand on his shoulder. It was her hand. It was the touch of reality amid the chaos. It was the touch of sorrow. It was the touch of love.

13

The ethereal reality that is Jesus' consciousness swirls and fades and reshapes itself. It is a face. It is the face—mostly the eyes—of Caiaphas: penetrating, accusing, denying eyes. Beneath the awful pain—the burning lungs, the cramping muscles, the throbbing wounds in his feet and wrists, the pulsating, sweat-soaked conflagration that is his skin—an anger glows in Jesus' soul. It is an anger that cannot be repressed because it is an anger that his swollen, bleeding mind cannot even recognize. He knows, yet does not know, that it exists.

"Hold him still!" Philip shouted.

"I *am* holding him," Simon shouted back as he fought to keep the halter rope taut. "If I didn't have hold of him, he'd be back to where we borrowed him from."

"We should have taken the old one," Nathanael said, struggling to place his spare tunic on the colt's back as the animal moved from side to side against the halter. "Damn!" he said, stepping back in disgust as the tunic slipped off and fell to the dusty earth yet another time. "This isn't going to work." Quickly he moved to pick up the garment when the colt's busy hooves gave him a brief opportunity.

"Why don't you tie it on?" Mary suggested from behind him.

Nathanael looked over his shoulder at her wordlessly. "You think maybe we haven't thought of that?" his expression said.

Jesus, standing next to Mary, was amused. How could he not be? This was one of those life experiences that you look back upon and wonder. "Did we really do that?" Here they were, perhaps a mile from the city walls, on a beautiful sunny morning, a steady line of pilgrims moving past them, most ignoring and avoiding the disciples who attempted to hand them palm branches and solicit their participation in the planned procession. And what was delaying the beginning of the joyful entrance? An uncooperative, unmanageable donkey.

"Whoooaa!" Simon hollered. The colt was winning, pulling Simon off his feet and dragging the fisherman sideways a short distance before Philip and Nathanael were able to push and shove the animal to a quivering halt. At that point, Simon was able to regain his feet, looking around as he did so, apparently in search of some kind of relief. Spotting Andrew nearby, he waved his brother over, in the process spooking the colt and setting off still another series of gyrations that yanked on the halter and almost caused the big man to fall again.

Andrew, solemn as always, moved cautiously toward his frustrated companions, Philip and Nathanael leaning their shoulders against the side of the uncooperative ass to prevent the animal from getting even further out of control and Simon pulling with both hands so that the donkey's nose was in the air, his ears back, and his neck braced in defiance.

"What do you want me to do?" Andrew asked after he'd stopped several paces from his brother.

"What do I want you to do?" Simon answered, his tone mocking Andrew's tentative offer of assistance. "What do I want you to do?" he repeated, this time almost in a shout. "I want you to take the damn rope and hold this demonic creature while I dust myself off!"

Philip, hidden from Jesus' view but presumably still pressing his shoulder against the animal's heaving side, called out, "This ass is possessed, Teacher. Cast the demon out!"

Jesus smiled in spite of a steadily increasing inner turmoil. As ludicrous as this situation had become, as laughable as this man-versus-beast contest might seem, there was a painful sadness pulsating and expanding within him. He could see the colt's fear radiating in concentric circles into the dusty glare of the morning. He could hear the buzzing terror and taste the acidic burn of panic.

"Why not try it?" Mary's voice was low and conspiratorial.

Andrew was quietly studying the shivering, snorting donkey, not replying to Simon's request. "Nice donkey," he said to the animal's nose. "I'm Andrew. I love you."

"Try what?" Jesus asked, understanding Mary's capricious intent but not ready to acknowledge it, amused but uncomfortable with his amusement.

"Order the demon out of the donkey," she said matter-of-factly. "What could it hurt?"

"When an unclean spirit leaves a person," Jesus said in response to Mary's suggestion, *"it wanders through waterless places in search of a resting place. When it doesn't find one, it says, 'I will go back to the home I left.'"*

"This isn't a person demon," Mary pointed out. "Donkey demons may be different."

"It then returns and finds the home swept and refurbished," Jesus continued, ignoring Mary's whimsical suggestion.

"Do you think I can hold him?" Andrew was asking Simon, taking a hesitant step forward.

"You damn well better!" Simon roared, setting off another struggle between men and animal.

"*Next,*" Jesus said, refusing to let go of his thought in spite of the tragicomedy taking place before them. "*Next, the unclean spirit goes out and brings back seven other spirits more vile than itself. They all enter and settle in there. So that person ends up worse off than when he started.*" He turned his head to look at Mary, intent upon keeping a straight face.

"Eight unclean donkey spirits," Mary said, her facial expression matching his. "And by then, you'll probably be on the poor beast's back."

"Temporarily," he said, raising his eyebrows in a case-closed manner before looking again at Andrew, who seemed to be still considering his options.

Finally Andrew moved cautiously closer and held out a tentative hand to take the rope.

"Set yourself," Simon warned. "Use both hands."

Andrew spread his feet apart and held out both hands, flinching slightly as the rope touched them and then closing his fingers around the hemp in a white-knuckled grip so that now both brothers were pulling against the arched neck of the colt.

Simon let go but remained where he was, obviously ready to grab the rope or Andrew, whatever was available, when the donkey made his anticipated lunge for freedom. Nathanael and Philip braced themselves. Even Jesus found his muscles tensing in spite of the fact that he had absolutely no intention of joining the struggle no matter what the poor ass might do. In truth, he was almost hoping that the colt would break free and run off. The pilgrims who continued to stream past them on the road seemed carefree and jubilant. A peaceful walk into New Town alongside them sounded good.

The animal's long ears twitched and then moved upward so that they pointed forward, seeming to examine Andrew with some sort of mysterious energy capable of judging this new tormentor's trustworthiness.

Gradually the spasmodic heavy snorts waned to a series of regular, wheezing breaths. The heaving rib cage of the animal seemed to relax, reduced to an occasional twitch of the skin as though shaking off a few pesky flies. The left hoof stomped once, followed by a shake of the head and a whiplike swish of the long tail.

Philip and Nathanael removed their shoulders from the donkey's left side and hesitantly stood up straight, looking at each other quizzically and then at Andrew, who, still using both hands, now found them tightly gripping a limp halter rope. He, in turn, looked at Simon. Simon, his sweaty face perplexed, looked to Jesus. "What's going on?" his expression asked.

Mary was the first to speak. "Why don't you go ahead and put your tunic on his back, Nathanael. Tie it on."

He turned his head toward her, hesitated, and then nodded.

They all watched in silence at Nathanael again placed his tunic on the donkey's quivering back and secured it in place.

"You cast out the demon. Right?" Mary said quietly to Jesus.

"Wrong," he said, watching as Andrew scratched the now tranquil donkey between the ears. "The donkey was terrified. Now he's not."

"God did something," she persisted. "Why would God care about a terrified donkey?"

Jesus sighed, his heart still racing, his stomach beginning to cramp. *"What do sparrows cost?"* he asked, turning to her and putting both hands on her shoulders. *"A penny apiece? Yet not one of them will fall to the earth without the consent of your Father."*

She seemed to consider the sparrows, looking not at Jesus but at the placid colt, at Nathanael tying the garments on the colt's back, at Andrew gently stroking the colt's nose and quietly reassuring him.

Jesus completed his thought. *"As for you,"* he said softly, *"even the hairs on your head have all been counted. So don't be timid; you're worth more than a flock of sparrows."*

She looked at him. "More than a donkey."

"More than a herd of donkeys."

"We all are."

"Each one of us."

"He's ready," Nathanael called to Jesus. "I think."

Jesus studied the waiting colt warily, then stretched his arms high over his head, enjoying the pull of the muscles in his back, the elasticity in his shoulders and arms. Apparently this ass-borne entrance into Jerusalem was really supposed to happen. Maybe it could be a quiet, friendly experience. He could talk to the travelers walking alongside, share the wonder of the great city as they moved toward the ponderous stone walls.

He allowed his arms to relax, lowering them gradually until they hung at his side, shaking them to release the tension. There being nothing to do at this point but mount his waiting steed, he turned and gave Mary a quick hug and then walked toward the donkey, whose ears now lay back against the top of his head as this new person approached.

Nathanael was waiting at the far side of the colt to give Jesus a boost, so it was necessary to walk around the beast at one end or the other. Andrew still stood at the head, both hands gripping the halter. The other end was clear except for the swishing tail and the potential of hooves kicking out dangerously. Jesus hesitated and then decided on the back end, giving the hooves a wide berth as he circled behind. Once that danger was skirted, it was a simple matter to move next to Nathanael, whose intertwined fingers formed a stirrup that Jesus could put his foot into and then lift himself upward.

It was done. The colt stood motionless, Andrew still talking to him to assure him that everything was okay. Jesus sat uneasily, wishing for something to hold onto, holding up his hands and looking at Philip to communicate his discomfort.

"Hold onto his mane," Philip suggested.

"I'll lead him," Andrew said. "You don't have to do anything but hang on."

Somehow the image of himself hanging on for dear life conflicted with the vision of a confident messiah galloping victoriously into the midst of cheering throngs celebrating their liberation. Jesus stared at Philip. "That's it?" he asked. "How impressive is that going to be if I fall off?" He pictured himself slipping slowly to one side and ignominiously plopping onto the dusty road with the donkey capitalizing on the opportunity to kick and pull free from Andrew's hold and gallop toward wherever he came from.

"Won't happen," Philip promised, stepping forward and giving the colt a slap on his haunch.

The donkey flinched and lurched forward, knocking Andrew aside and breaking into a trot. "Hey!" Andrew shouted, hurrying to catch up and grab the halter.

"Whoa!" Jesus hollered, bouncing in painful counterpoint to the donkey's jarring rhythm, wobbling, teetering, grabbing the mane with both hands, and finally righting himself as Andrew regained control.

Philip and Nathanael gave a shout of jubilation and ran ahead, waving to the disciples near the road, shouting instructions as they moved.

The plan was in place. They'd been cutting branches since yesterday afternoon, seemingly confident that people on the road would get caught up in the spirit of the festival and join the celebration whether they actually understood it or not. "Hosanna!" They were being instructed to cheer. "Save we pray thee!"

The donkey had settled into almost a gliding, forward and backward motion that Jesus found surprisingly easy to manage although it was impossible not to feel self-conscious about the image he must be presenting astride this ignoble beast—bare legs dangling, upper body leaning forward so that he could grasp the mane, head movement out of sync with the body movement as the forward and backward slide affected different parts of him in different ways. He hoped there would be no prancing Roman steeds with erect, confident, uniformed riders to create a contrast to his own undignified presence.

And even as he acknowledged his embarrassment, he chided himself for allowing his ego to intervene. This moment in time was not about him, he reminded himself. The kingdom of heaven was not about any man's ego. He was Yeshua ben Yusuf—Jesus of Nazareth. For reasons that he did not understand, he felt a responsibility to bring the concept of love to the people of Israel. For reasons that he understood even less, he found himself on this morning approaching the sacred city uncomfortably astride an ass.

They were on the road now. People he didn't know were stopping to watch him pass, waving palm branches over their heads, smiling, shouting "Hosanna". Some were spreading their branches—even their garments—on the road before him. It had been part of the plan to explain to anyone who asked, "This is the prophet Jesus from Nazareth of Galilee." Now, however, to Jesus it seemed that there was no need to explain anything. As Philip and Nathanael had predicted, the people were in a mood to celebrate. He released one of his hands from its death grip on the colt's mane and waved. Maybe he could do this! Maybe, in some mysterious way, he really was a messiah!

Simon appeared at his side, striding along, matching the colt's rolling gait. "Smile, Teacher," he called above the din of the crowd, looking up and grinning broadly. "Philip, says you've got to smile."

"Philip isn't the one who has to sit on this animal's backbone," Jesus called in return.

"It's only another half mile or so," Peter shouted. "Once we get near the wall, we're going to stop and find a place to build our sukkahs."

Jesus nodded, briefly calculated the length of time involved in getting to the northern wall, and then returned his attention to the crowd, still not smiling, he realized. After all, was a smile really appropriate? Would a messiah be smiling? John the Baptist's Messiah would not be. John's Messiah would be laying his axe at the root of the trees that did not bear good fruit, throwing the unworthy into the unquenchable fire. Surely he would not be smiling. His eyes would blaze with anger; his face would be hammered into iron rancor.

Jesus smiled softly! This messiah on the back of an ass was not John's Messiah. The smile broadened, spread to his heart, warmed his soul. He waved one hand. He waved both hands. He looked into the hearts of all who lifted their eyes to him. He made silent promises.

And the Hosannas, it seemed to Jesus, rose in intensity, reverberating, expanding and swelling and filling the morning sky with a chorus that was the song of God himself.

14

Words begin to form painstakingly across the soaked and battered papyrus that is Jesus' awareness: The buyer went plowing, discovered the treasure, and began to lend money at interest to whomever he wished.

Jesus groans.

As structures go, the sukkah was pretty sad. Sitting beneath the sparse layer of branches that they generously referred to as the roof, Jesus surveyed the twilight sky and let his attention wander from the discussion that was going on nearby. John had set off the debate by asking a perfectly logical question. "What's the point?" he'd asked, indicating with a wave of his hand the slopes of Bezetha covered with flimsy structures like their own.

"What's the point of what?" James had responded, not having followed the wave of John's hand.

"The sukkahs. This is a harvest festival. Why do we spend seven days sitting in a hut that doesn't even give us much shade?"

"We haven't spent much time sitting," Simon grumbled. "I'm sick to death of pinning people down and making them listen to my speech about the kingdom of heaven. I'll be glad to get out of here tomorrow."

"That's not the point either," John argued.

"The point," James grumbled, "is at the top of your head. Always you're worried about the point."

"So, did Moses and the Israelites live in sukkahs for 40 years?" He twisted his body to look at Jesus.

Jesus shrugged his shoulders. "Wasn't there," he said, not especially interested in the debate. "*Foxes have dens and birds have their nests,*" he added. "Maybe Israelites had their sukkahs." What he knew for certain was that Jesus the messiah had no place to rest his head.

"Of course they didn't," John said, answering his own questions. "They lived in tents. They weren't going to build a sukkah every time the Cloud of God told them to stop. Where would they get the branches in the wilderness? They needed shelter from the sun, not openings in the roof to stare at the stars through."

"How many Israelites do you think there were?" James asked.

John looked at him blankly. "How many?" he repeated. "What's it matter? Ten thousand...a hundred thousand...a million."

"So you think a million Israelites escaped out of Egypt carrying tents?"

That's when Jesus had tuned them out. It was not the Festival of Sukkot that concerned him. Whatever the significance of the past seven days, it had little to do with Moses or this year's harvest, at least as far as he was concerned. How many times this week had he been challenged by someone among his listeners? How threatened must they feel—Pharisee and Sadducee alike. They could not often agree with one another, but on the issue of Jesus and the kingdom of heaven, they obviously had united. When was the kingdom of heaven coming, someone at the back of the listening crowd had asked him this morning. "*It will not come by watching for it,*" he had answered. "*It will not be said,*

'Look, here!' or 'Look, there!' Rather, God's imperial rule is spread out upon the earth, and people don't see it." Predictably, this response had been met by a skeptical "Bah!" and a rambling harangue about observance of the Law and retribution for those who stray from its precepts. How many lives of misery had been needlessly prolonged because of one intractable bigot?

But that's the way it was. He was not going to be able to save everyone. They'd had a great week in spite of the antagonists. Now, except for one last strategic act, they could head back to Galilee, this time by the familiar route along the Jordan, maybe have a little fun along the way. It was that strategic act that was foremost in his mind right now. Philip and Nathanael didn't know anything about this one. Nobody did. Not even Mary. Their wonderful procession toward the city had been successful beyond their wildest dreams, but even it would take a back seat to what he planned for tomorrow. Well, planned wasn't quite the right word for it. He hadn't really planned anything. Somehow, though, like the procession, everything would fall into place.

"Teacher?"

He hadn't noticed Nathanael approach from sukkah Number Two. Number Two wasn't much of a name from a creative standpoint, but the process of giving a name to each of the huts as it was finished had gotten out of hand: Sheol, Eden, Pavilion, Tabernacle, Temple, Palace, Tent of Meeting were a just a few of the respectable suggestions. Accurately designating which was which and who was assigned to which was an exercise in futility anyway. Everyone, as Nathanael was doing now, moved freely between the three.

Darkness had overtaken New Town. A fire crackled outside Number Two, and hundreds of others had flared to life on the surrounding hills, but mostly the wavering, shadow-filled light was of little help in identifying faces. Nathanael was now just a hulking shape looming above Jesus. It was only through his voice that Jesus had recognized him. Interesting how the voice of each disciple had embedded itself in his memory. Each was unique, yet he would have been hard pressed to identify the qualities that made them different.

Nathanael used his feet to let other dark shapes next to Jesus know that he wanted to sit down, then waited while those shapes, shifting and grumbling, made a space available. "Teacher," he repeated once he was settled, "there's something that's been bothering me."

"You've come to the right place," Jesus answered. "I can add your problem to my own lengthy list."

John, one of the shapes who had moved to make room, joined the discussion. "You want to know where babies come from. Right?"

Nathanael ignored him. "It's not a problem," he said. "It's just something I've been thinking about."

Jesus waited.

"If the kingdom of heaven is already here, what happens when we die? I mean, is there someplace else to go? Is it better there than here?"

Conversation in the sukkah had ceased. A tension had intruded in the dancing darkness. A palpable energy, an energy of focused attention, vibrated in the shadows of the crowded hut.

"Nathanael," Jesus began, not really knowing what he was going to say, "I'm just a man like you. God is a Mystery. No human being knows the answer to your question."

Silence.

"But you must have thought about it."

"I *have* thought about it. I've thought a lot about it. Even though I know I can never figure it out, I think about it. Does that make sense?"

"Yes."

"I think…I think every man and woman who finds the kingdom of heaven in this life goes on to live forever—whatever *forever* is. I don't know how this happens. I don't know where it happens."

James's voice came from somewhere, maybe from the sky beyond the sukkah. It was the querulous voice of Everyman. "But, Teacher," James complained. "How is this fair?"

"How is it *not* fair?" Jesus countered.

"My brother and I…"

The hesitation generated a seeming profoundness to the words that followed.

"…Simon, Andrew…Mary…all of the disciples…have left our homes, our source of income, our families…to follow you, to teach others about the kingdom of heaven."

A silence of concurrence filled the hut even though James had not finished making his point. He was speaking what was possibly in the hearts of all of them even though some had not yet acknowledged this to anyone, even to themselves.

"How is it fair?" James continued. "A man is dying. In his final living moments, he recognizes the kingdom of heaven."

Jesus waited. It was easy enough to project James' thought to completion, but it was important that the words be spoken, that the disillusionment be given form and substance.

"This man…this man who has contributed nothing, receives the same eternal reward as one of us who has given so much for so long?"

There it was. Out in the open. A collective, soundless sigh radiated into the Jerusalem night.

Jesus allowed the sigh to dissipate before responding. "Will it surprise you," he asked, "if I answer with a story?"

No one spoke.

"I'll take that as a No," he said, pausing to collect his thoughts. It would be nice to tell the story right the first time. If he got it wrong, Nathanael would call him on it.

"Heaven's imperial rule is like a proprietor who went out the first thing in the morning to hire workers for his vineyard. After agreeing with the workers

for a silver coin a day, he sent them into his vineyard. And coming out around 9 a.m., he saw others loitering in the marketplace and he said to them, 'You go into the vineyard too, and I'll pay you whatever is fair.'

"So they went. Around noon he went out again, and at 3 p.m. and repeated the process. About 5 p.m. he went out and found others loitering about and said to them, 'Why did you stand around here idle the whole day?' They replied, 'Because no one hired us.' He told them, 'You go into the vineyard as well.'

"When evening came, the owner of the vineyard told his foreman, 'Call the workers and pay them their wages starting with those hired last and ending with those hired first.' Those hired at 5 p.m. came up and received a silver coin each. Those hired first approached thinking they would receive more. But they also got a silver coin apiece. They took it and began to grumble against the proprietor: 'These men hired last worked only an hour but you have made them equal to us who did most of the work during the heat of the day.' In response he said to one of them, 'My friend, did I wrong you? You agreed with me for a silver coin, didn't you? Take your wage and be satisfied! I intend to treat the one hired last the same way I treat you. Is there some law forbidding me to do with my money as I please? Or is your eye filled with envy because I am generous?'"

Within the undulating shadows of the sukkah, Jesus felt the voiceless protests of the men and women crowded around him, knew their unspoken sense of injustice, understood the internalized conflict of their egalitarian dreams. Equality, they'd come to believe, was at the heart of the kingdom of heaven. Anyone, they'd been teaching others, could experience the peace of God's love—simply by loving. Simply by Loving! Yet, somehow, their thinking brains were arguing…somehow, their logical human minds were insisting…somehow, those who worked hardest to bring love about were entitled to something extra. Somehow their sense of peace should be greater! Somehow their relationship with God must be more intense, more intimate, more…more glorious! It was only fair!

"James?" Jesus asked the shadows.

"Teacher?"

"What do you think?"

In the night-shrouded hills outside the city, distant human activity—tragic, comedic, tedious, anonymous life—intruded its perpetual voice.

"I don't know," James answered at last.

"It seems like you should be feeling good, doesn't it," Jesus suggested.

The physical presence within the sukkah seemed to shift and sigh intangibly.

"But you don't."

This time there was a response. "No."

"Neither do I," Jesus confessed as he struggled to his knees, groped for an unknown shoulder to steady himself, and finally managed to stand up. His legs were stiff and prickly, disinclined to hold his weight, but the sukkah was now closing in on him, confining him. The reluctant legs would have to function, to nudge and prod and squeeze their way past unseen living obstacles and into the freedom of the chill night air.

"Does that mean we've got it all wrong?" It was Nathanael's voice.

Jesus had begun one cautious step that now hesitated precariously. Why had he stupidly removed his sandals? Finding them now in this tangle of humanity would be impossible. His leading foot came to rest tentatively on what felt like an ankle; one balancing hand pressed against someone's head. "No," he answered without hesitation. This he was sure of. They didn't have it wrong. The kingdom of heaven was real, and they were a part of its reality.

"What it means..." he said. He was staring ahead, beyond the sukkah, at the dancing campfires spread out across the hills. How could he answer the questioning voice behind him? What could he say to all the silent voices asking the same question? His foot explored the dirt floor in search of stability. Finding it at last, he was able to bring the trailing foot forward and steady himself. "What it means," he repeated, "is that our tiny little minds are limited to dealing with tiny little concepts. Feeling good is about as far as our brains can take us."

Suddenly claustrophobic and queasy, he pushed his way past the bodies in the booth and moved toward the fire, stopping to stretch his arms over his head and take several deep breaths. His feet were cold. The thought of what he was going to have to do the next day sent an icy chill down his spine. Materializing in the flames of the fire, the stony, hate-filled face of the man who had challenged him that afternoon now unnerved him. Feeling good! He definitely did not feel good! But…my God! Was the kingdom of heaven all about having a full stomach? Was it possible to be at peace with himself—with God—and at the same time scared to death? Sick with disappointment? Suffocated by a sense of failure?

Mary was beside him. There had been no word, no touch, no peripheral flicker to let him know this. It was as though she had materialized, as though his need—through the darkness, through the jostle of competing bodies, through the interminable clamor of human emotions—as though his need had summoned her.

She put her arm around his waist. His arm responded, enveloping her shoulders, pulling her warmth close to him, her ear against his chest, sharing the steady voice of his heart.

"We have to get everyone out of here inconspicuously tomorrow," he said, the words reverberating in his chest more than being shaped by his mouth.

"What's wrong?" she asked.

"Nothing's wrong," he lied. No, it wasn't a lie. Things were going as they probably had to go.

"You sounded like something is wrong."

"No," he insisted, still gazing into the flames. "It's just time to head for home."

"Not that," she said to his chest. "Back in the sukkah. You said our tiny little brains could only think about feeling good."

"You heard that," he said stupidly. Obviously she'd heard it.

He felt her head nod against him.

"I should have kept my mouth shut," he said. They'd needed encouragement, and he'd offered only his own pain. Still, how could he be upbeat when the task God had given him was so clearly impossible? These were good men and women, but they simply were incapable of comprehending the kingdom of heaven except in physical terms. They knew all too well what it was like to be downtrodden. They were able to imagine an existence where there were no oppressors or oppressed, of an existence free of pain and trouble, yet they could conceive of such a heavenly existence only in terms of being perpetually happy—in terms of eating and drinking and playing and...possessing. Possessing! If some heavenly beings possess, must not some others *be* possessed? Can everyone be powerful? The kingdom of heaven couldn't be like that. The kingdom of heaven could not be driven by human needs.

"You had to tell them that feeling good doesn't necessarily mean..."

He felt her struggling to complete the idea. "Feeling good," he suggested.

She pulled away slightly and looked up at his face. "Yes," she agreed. "Feeling good doesn't mean feeling good...not all the time, anyway."

He met her gaze and smiled. "That would have been a big help," he said, certain that it would not have helped at all. "That would have made everyone..."

"Feel better," she grinned.

"That's right." Surprisingly, he was already feeling better. Incredibly, they were on the same page. The kingdom of heaven could be known even if it could not be explained. Maybe James and

Nathanael knew. Maybe everyone...well, now he was getting carried away.

He stood for some unmeasured time mesmerized by the flames, feeling good without analyzing the feeling, existing without thinking about existing, disappointed at last when some sound or movement—perhaps God himself—summoned him back to the moment. There were plans to be made, a strategy to be decided upon.

15

An abrasive screech penetrates the searing agony of Jesus' being. "What do I have to do with you, Jesus, Son of the Most High God?"

With difficulty, Jesus' eyes slowly open to the grayness of mid-morning. Within but beyond the image that gradually develops, dancing, multicolored lights make it difficult to discern what he is seeing. Nothing has changed: the forlorn hills, the rocky, desolate landscape that is Golgotha, the solitary figure waiting in the distant foreground. If he were able to turn his head he would see shredded human carcasses still clinging to the crosses next to his own, what carrion crows and scavenger dogs have not yet disposed of. To his left and behind him, he knows, the dark, impersonal walls of Jerusalem tell their never ending story of power and despair.

The sukkahs, womblike in the lightlessness of the body-heated night before, seemed pathetic in the chill sunshine of early morning. Building them had taken hours, but tearing them down took only minutes. Disposing of the now dry branches was a simple matter of dragging them to the nearest ravine and tossing them in.

Jesus sat on the ground, paying little attention to the dismantling process, focused, instead, on braiding three lengths of rope that he'd salvaged and tied to the trunk of a small tree. Most of the disciples had already dispersed, instructed to move eastward in groups of not more than two or three, some skirting the city on the north, some passing through the splendor of the Upper City and exiting through the Essene Gate on the southwest, others continuing to the maze of crowded, dusty streets of the Lower City on the southeast before exiting into the Kidron Valley. The objective, Simon had told them without giving reasons, was to get out of town without drawing attention to themselves, an easy task in a city whose population of perhaps 25,000 had swelled to three or four times that number during Sukkot. They were then to gather again in Bethany and wait for Jesus to join them later. Simon, Nathanael, James, and John would stay with Jesus and take down the sukkahs before losing themselves in the bustling anonymity as they, too, headed east.

Jesus watched with increasing frustration as his fingers struggled to keep the three strands of rope separate: right over center, left over right, center over left. The process couldn't be simpler. He'd watched Mary braid her long black hair without even being able to see what she was doing, carrying on a conversation at the same time. How could his stiff fingers be having so much difficulty? Gradually, though, the braid took shape. The next problem would be to secure it somehow when the braid was long enough—four or five feet should be enough. Simon had shown him how to do this, even a slip knot loop for Jesus to attach to the end. But Simon was a fisherman. He mended nets all the time. For him it was simple. Jesus' final knot would look like an unhealthy growth.

Mary's hair was still on his mind. *All* of Mary was on his mind. She'd wanted to stay, at first insisting that, whatever Jesus was going to do, she wanted to be a part of it. She'd sat down next to him and refused to leave with her assigned group. "I'll stay!" she'd said.

At first he hadn't argued, not really wanting her to leave, not really wanting to do what he had to do alone. How much easier it would be to have her at his side, to do what he had to do and then to have her with him as they blended in with the crowd, exited through the temple's Golden Gate, and scrambled down the Kidron bridge. It would be almost fun. It *would be* fun! They'd be laughing and remembering the shock they'd just inflicted and hurrying down the road through the valley exhilarated by a sense of danger and fear of pursuit.

Her voice had interrupted his fantasy. "So, then," she said, apparently mistaking his silence for assent. "It's all settled."

"No," he said quietly. Right over center; left over right. "Yes," he corrected himself, "it's all settled. You'll go with your group. I'll come along later."

For several seconds she'd been silent. "You want me to do that braid for you?" she'd asked.

He'd looked sideways at her and smiled. It was a thin smile. He'd felt its thinness, disliking its message. He *would* like her to do the braid. He'd like her to stay with him. The smile told her what his words could not. His attention returned to his fingers. Center over left. Right over center.

He remembered her standing up. There had been a finality about it, a sinking, awful sense of loss. "The sukkah's are down," she'd told him matter-of-factly.

He'd felt her eyes on his fingers, knew that she was willing those awkward fingers into deftness, hated that he'd rejected her help. "I guess you'd better get going then," he'd said.

There had been a long silence. "Okay," she'd said finally.

He'd sensed her moving away but had kept his eyes on his work, seeing, not his laboring fingers, but throngs of people on crowded streets, Mary and Nathanael entering the city through the Germath Gate, the Tower of Hippicus looming over them like a giant member of the Roman Guard. His mind had moved with them as they pushed their way through the Upper City toward the Essene gate—past the gleaming white marble of Herod's Palace, past the Dyers Quarter, past the imposing palace of Caiaphas.

Right over center; left over right; center over left. The fingers were remembering now, releasing Jesus to visualize his own way through the city. It wouldn't take long. The Tower of Hippicus would intimidate him as it probably had intimidated Mary and Nathanael. Instead of continuing south as they had done, however, he would turn east, the Upper Market pavilions on his left. Here would be the shops of the dealers in luxury goods: the distillers of expensive oils and perfumes, the master tailors and silk merchants, the goldsmiths and silversmiths, the dealers in ivory, incense, and precious stones. The Haesmonian Palace and the Palace of Annas, ominous and foreboding, would be on his right. Ahead of him, the sports Hippodrome would be seen in the distance and to the north of the Hippodrome, the Temple itself, its magnificent courts and cloisters looming heavenward from its position on the Temple Mount.

Enough! He yanked the braided rope and held it taut, cringing as he studied its amateurish irregularity. Three cubits, probably. Certainly sufficient for what he had in mind. Probably more than sufficient since he really had nothing particular in mind. He'd begun it on a whim and persisted out of some inexplicable urge. Perhaps it had been nothing more than nervous energy, something to do while he waited for the others to finish their task and be on their way. Now it was time to carry out his part in this plan that was not a plan.

He looped the strand that Simon had prepared for him around the end of the braid, pulled it tight to hold the strands in place, and then wound a single strand around and around and tied a knot. He used his knife to cut the loose pieces at the finished end and then, on hands and knees, cut the line that had been used to tie the other end to the tree. Actually, it wasn't half bad. He stood up, running his fingers along the length of the braid before grasping one end and cracking the other end against a larger tree nearby, surprised to realize that he had created a whip, the only whip he'd ever held, a whip that felt strong and good in his hand—frighteningly strong and good.

On the hills around him, most of the sukkahs were down, yet most of the people remained, probably planning to stay for another day or two, extending the festival, reluctant to let go of the emotional high and return to the drudging reality of their lives. The urge to confront them was almost irresistible. The passion to liberate them from the oppression of a tradition of fear of God burned now in his gut. He could take some time now to talk with at least a few of them. It was still early morning. There was really no hurry to get on with his mission at the temple.

His grip tightened on the braided rope in his hand. How foreign it felt, how contrary to his message of peace—yet how compelling. The Lord's instructions had not been tentative. The plan to disrupt the sacrificial ritual of the temple had not been a suggestion. It hadn't been a matter of the Lord asking him, "What do you think of this idea?" He'd known for several days that it had to be done. He'd known that this was the day that it had to happen. He could procrastinate all he wanted, but nothing would change. In frustration he snapped the whip against the trunk of the tree once again before picking up his backpack, surveying the scene around him one last time, and striding toward the Tower of Hippicus and the gate that would allow him to enter the city.

Once inside the gate, he changed his plan. On a whim, instead of turning east and passing through the Market Pavilions, he continued south past Herod's Palace almost to the southern wall and then turned left to head down the hill toward the Lower City. Almost immediately the streets became narrow and dusty, a maze of alleyways running uphill and down in every direction. At the bottom of the hill, the Small Market was crowded and busy, the streets lined with taverns and restaurants offering menus of salted fish, fried locusts, vegetables, soup, pastry, and fruit.

Jesus was comfortable here, forgetting about the braided rope that he carried in his hand, immersed in the clatter of hooves and the odors of cooking foods. While the presence of Roman guards throughout the city might well have tempered the joy and excitement of this festive time, no one seemed to notice them—no one else, at least. Probably this was because it was impossible for him to put his destination out of mind, impossible to ignore the ongoing mental projection of what was soon to happen. It was more than this, however. Even in the heat of the overcrowded marketplace, there was a tension, a chill numbing his spine and seeping outward across his back. Something was wrong. If he'd had hackles, they would be raised.

He stood in place, pushed and jostled by countless marketers moving past, and scanned the area as best he could. On some streets lined with one and two story houses, Jerusalem's craftsmen sat at work: weavers, dyers, potters, bakers, tailors, carpenters, and metalworkers—none concerned with him. In this particular area was the bazaar, where merchants sold fruits and vegetables, dried fish, sacrificial animals, clothes, perfumes, and jewelry. It was chaotic yet ordered. Everyone understood the process. Nothing seemed amiss. The only interest anyone seemed to have in him was that he was standing in the middle of the street, getting in the way.

Yet he was being watched. He was certain of it.

He began working his way north, a fairly steep climb toward the Temple Mount, his mind set now on the southern wall. The Huldah Gates, which he couldn't yet see, would provide access to the upper levels and to the Temple itself. He would have to get past the crowds of pilgrims, some with their own animals brought to sacrifice but most purchasing certified animals from the sellers. It was an incredible process. On the first day of the joyful Sukkot Festival alone, 30 bulls, rams, and lambs, and who knew how many hundred doves, would be sacrificed. This number decreased each day until the seventh, final day of the festival, when only seven bulls were sacrificed. But this was only a small part of the daily ritual of sacrifice that was carried on by hundreds of special priests, the kohanim.

It was a barbaric process, based on the premise that God demanded atonement for impurity and that this atonement had to take the form of specific types of sacrifices, including the burning at the altar of huge sections of calves, sheep, and goats. It was incredible to Jesus that intelligent people could venerate a God who would be pleased by senseless killing of animals. Was it rational to believe that God could be soothed by the aroma of burnt offerings on the altar?

"Friend!"

Still in the marketplace, Jesus found his way blocked by a man considerably taller than himself. Encountering such an obstacle was hardly noteworthy. There was no directional flow, no sense of order, in the Lower City. The scene was chaotic: hesitating, turning, sidestepping, fending off aggressive merchants, constantly searching ahead for an opening that might provide a fleeting opportunity to advance.

And now this large body—somehow hostile, somehow threatening—loomed in what he'd thought was a manageable path to his destination. Each attempt to move around this barrier as he'd done with countless previous barriers was purposely mirrored and defeated.

"Friend?" Jesus said, abandoning his effort to physically avoid a confrontation. He tilted his head back to look up at the sun-worn features of the man's shadowed face. Was this a problem? Was this what the nagging sense of foreboding was all about?

"I recognize the look," the man said. "You need an unblemished sacrificial bull."

His head still tilted, Jesus squinted past the face into the glaring sun above the Temple in the distance. "I brought my own bull," he lied. "It's already in line at the Sheep Gate."

The man turned his head as though he might somehow be able to see past the glittering gold roof of the Temple to the Sheep Gate beyond. Then he returned his attention to Jesus, turning so that he could put his arm around Jesus' shoulders and begin moving him through the crowds toward the Pool of Siloam, down the hill instead of up, east instead of north. "Name's Eleazar," he said. "Same as Aaron's son who took over as priest of the Israelites when Aaron died."

Jesus didn't reply. At least the guy hadn't claimed to be Abraham.

"The kohanim inspectors will never certify your bull," Eleazar said. "They work around the clock in shifts, selecting only the perfect beasts, only the fattest. No one ever brings a bull that gets approved. Or, for that matter, a sheep—or a dove. You know anybody who keeps sacrificial doves around the house?"

Jesus allowed himself to be guided through the crowd. Oddly, the way seemed easy, a path continuously opening up as they moved "You're right," he admitted. "I don't have a bull." He considered pointing out that he didn't need one, that the entire process from purchase to slaughter to burning on the altar was a shameless corruption of God's will. "How could I get one?" he asked instead, puzzled by his own question. What was going on here? Why was he humoring this predator? Why had he braided the rope into a whip if he wasn't going to use it to flail this thief and all the thieves who spent their lives corrupting the Temple?

The man's arm squeezed more tightly around Jesus' shoulders. "You've come to the right place," he shouted over the hubbub of the crowd. "Simplest thing in the world. You buy the bull from me, one the kohanim have already certified. That's step one. Step two, step three...every detail is part of God's perfect plan. Each priest has a special job: some provide wood, others the oil, others the fine wheat flour, others the spices, others bring the pieces of flesh for the burnt offering. And it's all done in silence. Hundreds of priests functioning in perfect harmony."

Jesus stopped, seething inside but under control, experiencing some sort of perverse satisfaction in deceiving the deceiver. "But how do they know which bull is mine?" he asked. "How can I be certain that I've atoned for my sins? How can God know which bull or sheep or goat or dove is mine? How can he know that the wonderfully pleasing aroma of burnt flesh has been made possible by me?"

Eleazar stared down at him in apparent disbelief.

"And if God doesn't know," Jesus persisted, "he's not going to know to forgive *my* sins instead of somebody else's." He pointed at a figure just climbing the steps of the crowded pool, the man's water-soaked tunic clinging to his fat body. "Maybe that guy over there will get credit for my bull."

Eleazar slowly shook his head. "It's not just your bull," he said. "Nobody can keep track of which bull you own a part of...which sheep...which dove. Do you have any idea how many animals get sacrificed up there? Thousands! Hundreds of thousands! The whole of the floor of the altar area is paved with stones. It all slopes down to special drains. The stones are slick with blood, all constantly being washed away by water from a natural spring that gushes up into the altar area."

Jesus stared toward the purification pool as Eleazar spoke, pulling free of the arm around his shoulders and maneuvering to the edge of the pool, feeling the big man's steps immediately behind him as he moved. For a while he watched the masses of people entering and emerging from the water. How clean could such water be? Even the

Siloam Spring could not possibly renew itself rapidly enough. Then he turned to look at his self-proclaimed benefactor. "I don't really need you, then, do I?"

"Of course, you need me," Eleazar insisted. "I sell you the animal. Without me, you don't get credit for the sacrifice."

Jesus pretended to consider that point, from this position, his view of the Temple Mount now mostly blocked by structures and by irregularities in the hill itself. He could only visualize the gates that he would have to enter to climb up to the outermost court, the Court of the Gentiles. "Why can't I just go on up and slip one of the kohanim a sheckle?" he asked without turning his attention from the area where he knew the Huldah Gates to be. "Why would that be different? I'd be buying a share of a bull." Now he looked up at the face of Eleazar. "That's all you're doing."

Eleazar scowled down at him.

Jesus forced a smile.

"You don't have any money anyway, do you," Eleazar grumbled.

"How can atonement have anything to do with money?" Jesus asked.

Eleazar stared over Jesus' head, apparently searching for another potential customer.

"The kingdom of heaven has nothing to do with cutting animals' throats!" Jesus continued. The braided rope felt alive in his hand. This seller of bulls was so pitifully corrupt that he couldn't recognize his own corruption. Was it possible that such a man—that the entire tradition of animal sacrifice—was so ludicrous that Jesus' anger was unwarranted, that the practice justified nothing more than scorn? And why even scorn? These people were comfortable with their God. Why not leave them to God? Why did he think it was his job to interfere with a practice that had been going on in one form or another for thousands of years? Why must he acknowledge the tradition at all?

The golden roof of the Temple glittered in the mid-day sun. Eleazar, the seller of animals he didn't own, had lost interest in Jesus and had already latched onto someone else in the crowd. An absurd sense of rejection settled over Jesus. Incredibly, he felt isolated, painfully alone in the midst of a teeming population, irreparably out of touch with humanity. Logically—rationally—one could not love one's neighbor—certainly not one's enemy—while demanding separation from that neighbor. Be like me, and I will love you. Relate to God as I relate to him, and I will affirm you. This could not possibly be God's plan! And yet…and yet, here he was, existing in a solitude so vast, so dark, so empty that God himself was not a part of it! Or…and this possibility was so incomprehensible that Jesus could not bring himself even to struggle with its magnitude…perhaps God *was* the solitude. Perhaps the kingdom of heaven was exactly that: being alone in the solitude that is God.

He didn't like it! Still, the deep inner voice that spoke to him about such things would not let him cast the notion aside. Idly he flicked the braided rope against the stone paving that surrounded the pool, diverted by the snakelike dance that his wrist movements could create. The rope snake writhed and lay in wait and struck in simulated attack, all at the whim of the hand, the unseen, omnipotent, unpredictable fingers that controlled its destiny. Writhe. Lurk in trembling stillness. Snap into deadly action. The process was hypnotic—irresistibly seductive. To the rope-snake, he was God. To God, he was the rope-snake. And as the rope-snake, poised to strike from his position on the rocks, he felt the chill of God race up his spine and resonate fearfully, icily, at the base of his brain. Could it truly be the Lord? He'd never experienced the kingdom of heaven in such a way before. A chill. An enervating sense of helplessness, of being observed and scrutinized and controlled.

No, it was something else. It could not be the Lord! Human eyes, not Godly ones, were examining him, measuring him.

The bellow of a shofar burst into his consciousness, his attention snapping immediately to the Temple Mount that was his destination and to his very reason for being here. What had happened to his focus, his passionate sense of purpose? Why wasn't he doing what he had come to do? The massive crowd exploded back into his consciousness: rivulets of sweat trickled down the small of his back beneath the sticky tunic, a cacophonous clatter of voices reverberated in his ears, the aromatic smoke of coal-darkened beef enticed his nostrils. Other than to remind him of his humanity, however, none of this was of any consequence. His destination lay in the direction of the shofar: the south wall of the Temple Mount looming in the distance, the opening in that wall that would allow him to enter and climb upward to the courts encompassing the Temple. There he would find the sellers of animals, the moneychangers profiting from the spiritual longing of people in pain. There, at the altar deep within the inner court, he would find the kohanim performing with precision the bloody ceremony of death.

16

Another screech shatters the silence. "Have you come to destroy us?"

Jesus' eyes lock shut. A bolt of terror crackles like lightning the length of his body even as he pushes with his legs against the nails in his heels to raise himself into a position that will allow him to exhale.

The demon is singing now, a jubilant, gloating croak, grating against the inside of Jesus' skull in punishing, repetitive lyrics that Jesus' battered mind cannot decipher. The hiss of foul air slipping past blistered lips becomes the background for a raucous chorus of abrasive voices that expand and expand: pounding, echoing, thumping, squealing in registers beyond human endurance.

For quite a while, no one noticed him. It had been easy enough to cross the Court of the Gentiles without attracting attention. The moneychangers at their tables were interested only in the task at hand: exchanging foreign coins for Jewish. The sellers of sacrificial animals were interested only in buyers. The pilgrims who had journeyed to Jerusalem had only one concern: being brought closer to God through the sanctification and sacrifice of an animal in their name. Most of them had been through the process many times. They understood the rationale: select an animal without blemish, bring it to the Temple, confess, watch the priests offer it, and eat it. They knew, as well, that the ritual, no matter how efficient the priests might be, could not function in that way for a hundred thousand people. So they exchanged their money at a loss, purchased an overpriced, theoretical animal, went through the ritual of prayer, and returned to their home.

So Jesus had experienced no trouble entering the Huldah Gates, climbing the widely spaced steps—constructed to encourage a contemplative, spiritual climb through the darkness of the tunnel, not an upward rush toward a counterfeit ritual—and zigzagging his way through the crowd of people negotiating in the shade of Solomon's Porch along the eastern wall. He'd entered the Women's Court and leisurely strolled through it and upward into the Court of Israel where perhaps 200 men were passionately petitioning the Lord for favor or forgiveness, probably none of them having any expectation of playing any personal role in this ritual even though the process was designed to include the man who provided the animal. The only essential players were the kohanim and the animal whose carotid arteries were to be severed.

Even the five steps upward and through the gate into the Priests' Court was negotiated without incident. Here, however, he stopped abruptly, struck by the magnitude of his transgression, awed by the priestly presence, stunned by an ambivalence throbbing with the grandeur of God yet rotting in the horror of humanity.

Now what?

Perhaps two dozen kohanim—not the 700 that Eleazar had described—robed in blood-splattered linen garments down to their ankles, moved about in a ritual that seemed choreographed and eternal in its efficiency. Those who passed by closest to where he stood had to be aware of his intrusion, but there was no reaction. Indifference filled the court like the overpowering aroma of burning fat.

He forced his mind to slow down, to examine, to consider alternatives.

A ramp at his left led up to the base of the altar, which may have been as much as 50 cubits square. The altar itself stood at least twice Jesus' height, a huge horn extending from each corner. Next to the ramp was a pool of water, a stone laver, making it possible for the priests to wash their hands and feet before making a sacrifice.

To his right, at the opposite side of the altar, was the blood-soaked area where the animals were slaughtered, the shambles. Two rows of rings were attached to the stone floor for the purpose of restraining each animal before the throat was cut and the skin stripped from the body. A constant flow of water washed across this elevated area and apparently drained at some point beyond the altar. Where it went, Jesus had no idea.

On each side of the altar Jesus could see that separate rooms ran along the north and south walls of this western half of the Temple. Probably, he guessed, each chamber was designed to accommodate a different aspect of the sacrificial process: maybe a place to salt the hides, perhaps a room to butcher the animal and rinse the innards, probably a place to store the vast quantities of firewood that were needed.

Having viewed the Temple from the outside on previous visits to Jerusalem, Jesus knew that there were upper stories of interconnected rooms. He knew, as well, that beyond the altar and beneath these upper rooms was the Holy Place, where only priests were admitted. Beyond the Holy Place was the Holy of Holies, the two areas separated by only an ornately decorated fine linen curtain. Jesus had always envisioned this curtain billowing softly in a perpetual breeze, a breeze not so much sent by God but, in fact, the very essence of God. This vision, of course, flew in the face of the tradition that not even an image of God—certainly not God himself—had been in this place since the destruction of the first temple: no Ark of the Covenant, no stone tablets, no Mercy Seat, no Presence of God. And how much sense did that make? How could a place be holy if God was not there? Even more self-evident, how could there be any place where God was not? No one except the High Priest could enter the Holy of Holies, and even this could happen only once a year when the blood of the Great Day of Atonement was sprinkled on an unhewn stone.

The korbanot choreography continued with a wordless military precision, determined by a cadence that everyone seemed to hear but that no one voiced. Carrying a hind quarter of a bull, two kohanim passed silently in front of Jesus and headed toward the ramp on his left. Three others tugged and pushed a large ram toward one of the iron rings while two long-robed priests waited wordlessly, knives in hand. Several priests moved into and out of the laver, each pausing only briefly to bend down and soundlessly cleanse his hands. Purposeful shadows shifted within the chambers to Jesus' left and right. The glow of the coals high above Jesus' line of sight reflected brightly off the ceiling tiles. Like the melody of a stream dancing over pebbles—a dragonfly drifts on the surface of the pond—the incessant spring water rose from mysterious depths and trickled downward again into streams and washed unceasingly over the stone floor. The sweet aroma of blood, of pulsating life and decaying death, hung heavy in the air, within but beyond the miasma of smoke and burning flesh and excrement.

His imagination could see and hear it clearly: his braided rope cracking like a whip, shattering the wordless cadence of the ritual, snapping the back of time itself. His arm would swing over his head. The rope would arc and the rope-snake descend toward the base of the altar. A rock-rending, temple-splitting, deafening crack would signal

God's cosmic displeasure. The billowing curtain would rip from top to bottom. The deserted Holy of Holies would cave in on its own emptiness. In shock, the entire sacrificial process would snap and cease as the godless force that turned the wheel of sanctimony broke and disintegrated.

The vision was improbable, almost hysterical, Jesus knew, yet there was great satisfaction in indulging his fancy. God could certainly destroy the Temple. That the means of destruction might be Yeshua ben Yusuf and a braided rope was a credible possibility for a God who could flood the earth or inflict pestilence upon half a million Israelites or use the blasts of trumpets to crumble the walls of Jericho. Suppose that David, because his only weapon was a slingshot, had declined to do battle with Goliath? God had brought Jesus of Nazareth to Jerusalem for the Festival of Sukkot. For no apparent reason, God had helped him braid the rope, had sent him alone to the Temple. Perhaps the braided rope was his slingshot.

With a weary whoosh and a splat, the rope-snake smacked unimpressively against the film of moisture washing over the stones.

Nothing changed: water rippled over stones; warm blood flowed from severed jugulars. The mute dance of the kohanim—killing, flaying, offering, purifying—continued without interruption.

"The kingdom of heaven is Now!" Jesus screamed. The Temple had not collapsed. Well, that was God's choice. Jesus felt no embarrassment, no sense of failure. How was anyone ever to know when he was an instrument of the Lord and when he was just doing his own thing?

"The Lord is in the Holy of Holies!" he shouted almost maniacally. "Everywhere in this Temple!" He paused, stunned by his own outburst, unsure of what to do next. "Everywhere!" he screamed.

The kohanim had stopped moving now, some glaring at him, others looking around as though hoping that someone else would do something. At least he had their attention. There was something very unnerving about seeking attention and not even being noticed.

"The Lord hates your sacrifices!" Jesus shouted, his voice now slightly more under control. On his left and right, priests were moving into his range of vision as they came out of the chambers to investigate the disturbance. Still not hundreds of priests, but many. There was no way to know if others still labored in the more distant chambers, if others were resting, awaiting their turn to work. For the first time, he noticed the animal sounds that must have been present all along: bleats, what sounded like moans, the whistling, frantic flutter of hundreds of caged doves from somewhere beyond his view.

Methodically his fingers retrieved the rope, twisting it into a loop as he studied the reactions of the kohanim. They didn't seem inclined to dispute his words or to physically remove him from their Court. They seemed confused, immobilized by this interruption. Their indecisiveness, Jesus was certain, did not indicate that they were considering his words. Quite possibly his message made no sense to them at all. More than likely, they did not feel rebuked but merely disoriented. In their minds, the sacrificial ritual was a celebration of the cycle of life and death. It was no more to be questioned than was the rising and setting of the sun.

"You've turned the Temple into a marketplace," Jesus told them, his voice now under control. "You've become seekers of profit. Men come to you to find peace, but you give them blood."

No response. No reaction. Even the continuing animal sounds suggested bewilderment. The Priests' Court, the Temple Mount—God himself—seemed to be waiting for something more to happen. When it did not, when the Temple Mount did not explode in a holocaust of smoke and flame, as the water of purification continued to bubble peacefully upward and spread itself across the stones, the wheel of death ground gradually into motion once again. The priests who had emerged from the chambers one by one turned and disappeared from view. A priest standing in the laver bent to wash his hands. Two halfway up the ramp resumed their climb, carrying the dripping leg of a large animal to the altar.

Jesus watched in silence. Was that going to be it? Had God directed him to this place knowing—certainly knowing—that the impact of his effort would be less than minimal? Had he failed? He knew better than that, yet it was impossible not to think of what had just happened as failure. There it was—killing, flaying, offering, purifying—nothing had changed. What was the point?

He scanned the area again, no doubt for the last time, frustration mounting, a strong sense of failure settling over him in spite of his self-reassurances. Was it time to leave the city and head for Jericho? Was this the culmination of his ministry? Could he return to Galilee—maybe even Nazareth—and resume a quiet life of…? Of what?

17

Silence! Empty, sterile, lifeless silence! Jesus hangs in vacant, agonizing anticipation.

Exhausted muscles fight for life. Gradually he edges upward against the grain of the wood.

This time it is a mocking roar. "Command us, Jesus of Nazareth!"

Soundless vacuum.

"Rebuke us!"

He turned, his back now to the altar, and gazed through the gate that separated the Priests' Court from the Court of Israel. Theoretically, most of the men whom Jesus could see through this opening should have been mounting the five steps and positioning themselves so that they could lay their hands on the head of the victim as the throat was cut. In practice, however, this requirement was impractical. Who knew which animal belonged to which man...to which men? There was no way to coordinate this operation. As a result, each person who had paid for a sacrifice stood in the Court of Israel accusing himself in his prayers for whatever length of time he felt was appropriate. Then he would depart, usually through the gold and silver plated Gate of Nicanor, down the 15 steps that led to the Women's Court and through that court to any one of several gates that would return him to the Court of the Gentiles. No one doubted that the Lord was keeping track, hand on the head or not, multiple purchases of the same animal or not.

It was ridiculous! The priests of the Temple were using Mosaic Law to defraud the people! In return, the people were either very gullible or happy enough to be defrauded. Maybe both. Hardly anyone could read, and, even if they could, the Law wasn't organized and recorded in any obtainable form. Presumably it was all in the Books of Moses. Somewhere. At least the priests and scribes said it was. And even that information was mostly unavailable. Almost everyone's knowledge of the Law was based on what his family or his neighbor told him, not on any formal learning process.

Jesus strode through the gateway and stopped on the top step. "What are you people doing?" he shouted.

A few men looked up but most remained focused on their prayers, their bodies moving rhythmically, their heads bobbing up and down, their hands beating against their chests.

"You're trying to buy forgiveness!"

A few more heads stopped bobbing and looked up at Jesus curiously.

"They've turned God's house into a marketplace!" He snapped the rope against the hand rail, this time achieving a whip-like cracking sound.

A man entered from the Women's Court. Three others turned and departed. Bodies twitched, heads bobbed, hands thumped chests.

Jesus descended the five steps two at a time, the rope-snake twisting along the stone floor behind him, and pushed his way through the crowd. Enough was enough! No one in this court was going to listen to him. When you're driven by guilt and shame, you're going to listen to the guy who promises traditional relief, not to a crazed stranger who insists that you're going about the business of atonement all wrong. Pay your money. Say your prayers. That was why the Lord gave us priests.

Most of the men in the crowd endured contact with him without seeming to notice, but just before he reached the huge gate that would allow him to descend to the Women's Court, he bumped heavily into one large man, eliciting an angry curse. Another reached out a grasping hand that Jesus narrowly avoided. Immediately he was clear and at the top of the 15 steps of the semicircular stairway that led downward into the confusion of the Women's Court: doves for sale, moneychangers at their tables, both men and women moving about with apparent purpose, others sitting on benches conversing. On three sides, the size of this Court was defined by a covered porch, perhaps 40 cubits wide. This structure, Jesus knew, ran the length of the Temple, separated at intervals by nine gates in the shape of towers. The three gates in the Women's Court, on the north, east, and south sides, would allow him to exit when he—when the Lord—was ready. It didn't really have much to do with his own readiness. He was ready now. There was no point in talking to any of these people. At the same time, he knew that his mission wasn't finished. There was something more to do. Just what that something was, he didn't know.

He reached the bottom step and looked to his left where a large chamber had been built. In this room, he knew, the purified lepers were able to bathe before presenting themselves to the priests. A similar chamber in the right corner of the Court was for oil and wine to be used for the drink-offerings. To his left, in a third chamber in the east corner, priests who were unfit for other than menial services on account of bodily blemishes separated worm-eaten wood from that destined for the altar. In the southeast corner, a fourth chamber was a place for those who had fulfilled the vow of Nazarites to shave their heads.

Jesus hesitated and then headed to his left. Along the wall between the stairway and the lepers were 13 containers where charitable contributions could be placed. Each was wide at the bottom and narrow at the top like a trumpet, and each was marked for a specific purpose. Though he was well acquainted with these containers, Jesus paused to read what was written on each: Trumpets I and II were for the half-shekel Temple tribute for the past year. Women who had to bring turtledoves for a burnt and sin offering could drop the equivalent in money into Trumpet III. Theoretically, this money was taken out daily and a corresponding number of turtledoves offered. Theoretically! Who except the Lord himself knew? Trumpet IV served a similar purpose but for young pigeons instead of doves.

Jesus moved to Trumpet III, put his hand on the narrow top and pulled. It didn't take much effort to topple it. The crash of it hitting the floor was minimal and attracted little attention.

He did the same with Trumpet IV, attracting some indication of surprise from those in the immediate area but not stirring up any major clamor of protest. Mostly, people didn't notice.

Trumpets V through XIII—money to pay for wood to use in the Temple, for incense, golden vessels for the ministry, money a person might have left over from the cost of various offerings—clattered to the floor in succession.

Now he'd been noticed. Angry voices of protest arose. People who'd been in other areas of the court were moving to investigate. Strangely, Jesus thought, his mind racing yet focused, no one was moving to restrain him.

He looked around. What next? Should he shout his message as he'd done unsuccessfully in the Court of Israel or the Priests' Court? There was no point in any of this if no one knew why he was doing it? Still, it seemed futile to explain. Maybe if he could sit down with just a few and discuss the matter quietly. It was difficult to get his thoughts in order. He felt driven and out of control. "The kingdom of heaven," kept repeating itself in his mind. "The kingdom of heaven." What could the kingdom of heaven possibly have to do with starting a riot in the Temple?

"Everybody out!" he screamed. "The Scriptures say, 'My house is a house of prayer.'"

He raised his arms over his head and looked upward, intending to indicate the walls and columns of the Temple itself but distracted and stirred instead by the cloud-streaked brilliance of the afternoon sky.

Lowering his gaze, he scanned the faces of the gathering crowd before shouting once more. "You've turned the Lord's house into a marketplace!"

He waved the rope-snake over his head and strode toward the midst of the now rather large crowd that had arched itself around him. The people retreated to allow him to pass. In the middle of the opening, he stopped and used his rope to point back to the line of trumpets he'd toppled. "The Lord is not moved by your money!" he shouted. "Atonement is not for sale!"

With no clear plan as to what to do next, he turned and moved further into the retreating crowd, finding himself suddenly clear of them and encountering, instead, several moneychangers at their tables. The closest one stood up defensively and backed away. Jesus strode forward, set himself, and brought the braided rope furiously down onto the top of the table, scattering coins across the marble floor, startling himself and eliciting a wail of protest from the man who had abandoned his station.

Wiping perspiration from his forehead with the back of his hand, he moved to the next table. The crowd was a blur now. He was only distantly aware of shouts or screams. His leg crashed into another table, surprising him, unleashing a surge of dizzying hot anger. In response, his hands grasped one edge and lifted with a violence that flipped the table onto its side and sent coins clattering.

He stared, hardly seeing, past a heaving, formless shape that he only vaguely identified as human beings. Hazily he imagined himself outside—through the entrance, down the steps, beyond the low wall that marked the limits of non-Jews and the unclean. Outside became his destination.

A moneychanger to Jesus' right now stood, knocking over his chair and, using his hand and forearm, frantically attempting to gather his coins into a bag. Though he wasn't seeing the man clearly, though the man was doing nothing that could be interpreted as hostile, Jesus' rage exploded. The rope swooshed into action, this time in a sideways arc that ripped the bag from the man's hand and sent the money flying.

A few uncertain steps put him in the midst of a stack of cages containing turtledoves. The cages with the terrified birds still inside toppled and crashed to the floor. "Sorry," he said, addressing the birds, not the irate merchant who berated him while attempting to retrieve the scattered cages.

Jesus attempted to take in the scene. Breathing heavily, overcome by a pulsating heat and a dizziness that left him weak and disoriented, he leaned on a table and attempted to evaluate the situation. For reasons that he could not bring his mind to bear on, no one had yet attempted to halt his rampage. He sensed the people closer now, imagined the circle of hostility tightening around him. Someone…someone buoyed by the presence of a gathering crowd of angry others…perhaps many someones…would soon find the courage to grab him, to knock him down, to punish him with blows and kicks and angry words.

He looked again toward the south wall, perplexed by an irrational sense that safety lay in that direction. The Roman Guard was out there, soldiers with emphatic instructions to maintain control. At the same time, this inexplicably passive crowd in the Women's Court could not be expected to restrain itself much longer. Outside or inside, he was cornered. He was about to be overpowered, pummeled, and…and what? Dragged outside the city and stoned? Turned over to the Romans? Carcass-clad crosses along the road outside the city flashed through his consciousness.

Through the burning haze that was his mind, he began to react, not logically and strategically but instinctively. He forced himself to straighten up and stand tall. It was his audacity, his cloudy mind suggested, that had protected him thus far. There would be no shortage of suddenly courageous defenders of the Temple if he showed weakness. Self-preservation, whether he honored it or not, was driving him now. He forced himself to turn slowly in a circle, to direct a steady, confident gaze toward the men who now surrounded him, to intimidate them, to use the piercing authority of his probing eyes to convince them that he was in control, that any effort to interfere on their part would be a mistake that they would regret.

His thoughts began to take shape now. This was no longer a frenzied, out of control act of defiance. It was becoming, instead, a plodding analysis of purpose. Love your enemies. Turn the other cheek. God's words throbbed in his head. What better time to make the point? These people would listen. They would turn their lives around. They would find the kingdom of heaven. That's what this was all about! This is why the Lord had sent him to the Temple today—to get people's attention.

No, his survival instinct argued. No, this was the time to back off—without allowing it to seem like a retreat. He would walk calmly past the tables of the moneychangers, past the line of men, any one of whom might explode in anger and knock him to the floor, past the women who had collected in nervous groups behind the men, to the gate on the south wall. And then…?

Teach or retreat? Either way, there would be consequences. Probably he should be examining his options, making choices, yet he was unable to direct his thoughts further. And did it really matter whether or not he struggled with choices? God had put him here. Today's events and their consequences may have been worked out long before now. He would do what he would do. This moment would play out the way it played out.

It wasn't far. The porch containing the gate was perhaps 20 cubits—15 steps, 15 confident steps, 15 defiant steps—away.

He took two hesitant steps, recognized them as hesitant, and stopped. Already he could feel the approach of the angry men behind him. He turned. Had they moved? He wasn't certain. "*The kingdom of heaven is like a woman who was carrying a jar full of meal,*" he said quietly.

Except for the flutter of the still-frightened doves and the soft weeping of a woman to his left, the court was eerily silent.

Jesus swept the faces of the men nearest him with his eyes. "*While the woman was walking along a distant road,*" he continued, "*the handle of the jar broke and the meal spilled behind her.*"

He turned, took a step toward the gate, and stopped again. "*She hadn't noticed a problem,*" he said in the direction of the gate, his voice stronger now, assertive. "*When she reached her house, she put the jar down and discovered that it was empty.*" He looked back over his shoulder. "Empty!" he shouted.

There was no reaction, no indication that they had even heard the story, let alone understood it.

He returned his attention to the gate and began striding toward it, counting his steps, focusing on his destination, attempting not to think about what was happening behind him. His ninth step took him to the entryway that led to the gate. It would take that many more to reach the outside. Voices behind him made it clear that the crowd was coming to life. He could feel the bravery escalating behind him as the power of superior numbers blended with the people's sense of indignation. How much longer before they would be coming after him?

Bravado had gotten him this far, but it wasn't going to get him much further. Still, it seemed to be all he had.

He strode through the portico as resolutely as possible, hesitating at the gate for an instant to take in the scene. As he'd known it would be, the Court of Gentiles was alive with activity. Safety lay in getting down the 12 steps and past the stone wall, the soreg, that encompassed the Temple. If he could blend with the mass of people and work his way south toward the Royal Portico, he would be okay.

Taking two steps at a time, dodging people coming up, he loped downward, his eyes on his feet even as his mind gazed southward to where the massive columns and roof of the Royal Portico loomed in shaded splendor.

On the bottom step, he stopped, glancing over his shoulder at the gate behind him, reassured by the sight of people entering the Court but no one coming out. Was it really going to be this easy? Were they not going to pursue him?

He decided to turn to his right. It was possible that Levites or Roman guards from the Antonia Fortress had already been alerted. It was possible that he would be arrested the moment he passed through the opening in the soreg. It might be smarter to move to his right along the narrow area between the wall and the embankment that slanted upward to the Temple. There were other gaps in the wall, one at each of the nine gates that accessed the various courts, all little used because almost everyone entered by way of the Court of Women. For that matter, it now occurred to him as he walked, there was no reason to risk using any of the entrances. The soreg wasn't a high wall. To verify this fact, he turned his head slightly as he hurried by. He could see the faces of people on the other side. Beyond them, the Royal Portico beckoned seductively as a place of refuge.

He stopped and looked back to check for pursuers. A further check of the court on the other side of the soreg gave him no reason to suspect danger. Deciding that now was as good a time as any, he put his hands atop the stone wall and used his arms for leverage as he jumped, pulling himself up until he could sit on the top and then, with a backward push of his hands, dropping down on the other side. He landed on his feet but fell forward onto his knees before scrambling upward and heading for the nearest group of people. Now, if he could just blend in, if he could keep moving toward the Royal Portico without attracting attention.

18

Her face…soulful eyes behind dark hair cascading to her shoulders…her face persists—brightening, fading, brightening, fading—deep within the awareness that endures beyond awareness.

Her face…heavy brows narrow above questioning eyes.

Even now, as death envelops him, he is desperate to explain, to provide answers, to help her understand that which cannot be understood. But the awful pain persists. The questions themselves are illusive. Frustration swirls within frustration. Words flash and disappear, consumed by thunderous, roiling black mind-clouds—peace, love, joy, mercy, righteousness—words that lay bare the great mystery. He has owned these words, given them light, rejoiced in their truth, but now they streak, unattainable, across the stormy sky of his agonizing impotence.

The arms wrapped around him from behind, pinning his own arms to his body, immobilizing him completely. His eyes locked him into darkness. A flash of fear crackled the length of his body. His brain, instantly numbed, reverberated with a silent scream.

"Can't you read the signs on the wall?"

The arms had a voice. What did the voice want to know?

"No foreigner is to enter within the balustrade and embankment around the sanctuary," the voice read to him.

He heard the words, but they made no sense. Foreigner?

"Whoever is caught will have himself to blame for his death which follows."

Thoughts were forming hazily now. His brain was assembling questions. What were the questions? They were important ones, he was certain.

"Teacher," the voice said.

He opened his eyes and attempted to turn his head to look at the voice. Incredibly, he knew the voice. Incredibly, it was Nathanael's voice. It was Nathanael's arms that held him motionless.

Several men edged their way past, apparently not noticing anything unusual. The chatter and commotion of a thousand people blended into his consciousness as a single sound, like the distant hiss and roar of ocean surf.

From in front of him, another voice broke in. "Yeshua," the second voice said, its throaty warmth suggestive of rich red wine and a warm fire. "Yeshua," Mary repeated, relax and do as we tell you."

It was a warm spring morning. They were all together, sitting near the Upper Jordan. It was the first time he'd heard her speak. "In Magdala…" she had begun, her honeyed voice a counterpoint to the steady hum of life that filled the warmth of the morning. "…in Magdala we are fish processors."

They were on the road to Hazor. Mary's mischievous call had added laughter to the trek. "It was John," she'd shouted. Nearly choking, he'd stifled a laugh and then acknowledged and released it. Mary's husky, rolling guffaw exploded in response. She fell against him and let him wrap his arms around her and support her and laugh deliciously, silently, with her.

"Am I different from you," Mary had asked the Samaritan woman at the well, "because for 700 years we've made no effort to understand one another. Neither of us is a Jew." She sipped again from the cup. "Both of us are Jewish," she added.

"Relax," she'd told him just now. At this moment…at this most precious moment…with Nathanael's arms still around him and the stifling shock of capture frozen in his memory, he was separated by a lifetime from any control over his thoughts, from any rational sense of his emotions, from any possibility of determining what he would do next. He was helpless.

"You're going to have to carry me out of here," he managed to say.

There was no honey in Mary's reply. "Come on, King of the Jews," she scoffed. "You can walk on water…you can shuffle your way through this mob."

He felt his lips' weak attempt to shape a smile.

Nathanael's arms relaxed their hold, and he moved to Jesus' side. "Put your arm around my waist," he instructed. "Lean against me."

"Follow me," Mary said as she turned away from him. "Act like you're feeble." She began to work her way through the crowd.

"I *am* feeble,' Jesus called after her. His legs were wobbly. How was that possible? Only a short time ago he'd been knocking over tables, striding down steps, climbing over walls.

Mary was twisting and turning her way east, not south. Beyond her, the columns of Solomon's Porch stretched along the eastern wall of the Temple Mount, not as massive as the Royal Portico but impressive nevertheless. In the middle of that wall, a gate led out to the Kidron Bridge that connected with the Mount of Olives beyond the valley.

"There'll be a tax collector and guards at the gate," Jesus said to Nathanael. "We'll never get past them."

"She's not heading for the East Gate," Nathanael answered.

"Why not go south?" Jesus asked. "I came in through the Huldah tunnel. We can go back out that way."

"We'd still be in the city."

He thought about that. Eventually they would have to pass through one of Jerusalem's gates. The longer they waited to do it, the more likely it was that the guards would be alert and watching for them. But, if not the East Gate, where?

Mary was angling to the left now, checking back over her shoulder as she moved, apparently wanting to stay far enough ahead of them to avoid the appearance of their being together, but not wanting to lose contact.

Jesus' legs were functioning well now. He kept his arm around Nathanael's waist, more because he was reassured by the contact than because he needed support. How incredible it all was! They'd stayed in the city instead of heading for Jericho as he'd instructed. They'd watched him, followed him. Had they been in the Court of Women to watch his tantrum? He hoped not. He didn't feel good about what had happened, God's plan, or not.

They were heading north, the east entrance to the Court of Women on their left. The crowd was thinner here.

"The Sheep Gate," Nathanael said, letting his arm drop from Jesus' waist. "You okay to walk?"

Jesus nodded. Actually, he was feeling good now. An elation was growing inside, an exuberance that was energizing and clean.

The Sheep Gate! It made sense. No one would be paying attention. A steady flow of animals for sacrifice moved through the gate all day, especially during the festivals. No one was likely to ask questions.

As they approached the north wall and the gate, Mary dropped back to join them. Together the three of them strode brazenly along the line of animals being led in the other direction, Mary in the middle, one arm around each man's waist. To their left, in the northwest corner of the

Temple Mount, the Antonia Fortress, usually ominous and threatening, seemed almost friendly.

At the gate, Mary dropped her arms and followed the two men through, each of them nodding a casual greeting to a kohanim who was leading a huge bull in the opposite direction.

As he and Nathanael cleared the wall, Jesus stopped, took a deep breath, and gazed joyfully eastward. Nathanael continued for several steps before stopping and looking back. Below them, on their right, the hill sloped downward into the Kidron Valley. On the other side, the Mount of Olives basked lazily in the afternoon sun, its summit slightly higher than the Temple Mount where they stood. It was too soon to celebrate. There was still much that could go wrong. Still, it felt deliciously good to be outside the city. Nathanael grinned. Jesus matched it and turned to give Mary a hug, only then realizing that she was no longer close behind them. Instead, she had stopped in the shadow of the gate and was carrying on a conversation with one of the priests.

Restraining a flutter of nervousness in his stomach, Jesus took a few steps toward the gate before stopping to figure out what was happening. Mary was reaching out tentatively to touch the back of a sheep that hadn't yet begun its final walk. As Jesus and Nathanael watched, she tilted her head to look innocently up at the tall priest who held a rope attached to the sheep. She seemed to be asking him a question.

The faintest trace of a quizzical smile formed on the priests' lips. He turned his head to look at the man next to him in what was a large group of seemingly restless, impatient sheep and bored kohanim, and then looked back at Mary. His reply, whatever it was, was brief.

Mary seemed satisfied with the response, she and the priest and the sheep silhouetted against the sunlit background of the Court of Gentiles and the Temple. At last she looked toward Jesus, grinned, turned her head to say some final word to the priest, and then moved—

to Jesus it almost seemed like a skip—on through the gateway. Catching up with them, she put one arm around each and nudged them toward freedom.

Curious as to what Mary could possibly have had to say to the priest—what could possibly have motivated her to risk their being questioned and taken into custody—Jesus resisted her nudge, holding his ground until she looked at him and then questioning her with raised eyebrows.

Her response was to tug on their arms and then let go, walking ahead to where the hill began to drop away toward the Kidron Valley and starting down, not bothering to follow the worn pathway that switched back and forth down the barren limestone descent.

Jesus watched in silent amusement, knowing that Mary would not stop, would not look back. It would serve no purpose to call to her, to suggest that they avoid the rocks and thorns and loose gravel of the direct path to the bottom of the hill. It occurred to him that he and Nathanael did not have to follow her. They could follow the path. He looked at Nathanael, knew that Nathanael was considering the options just as he was doing, knew that Nathanael would make the same choice as he.

Down the hill they plunged.

"Hold up, Mary!" Nathanael called after her.

She stopped and looked back, grinning broadly.

Jesus looked ahead briefly and grinned in return before putting his head down and focusing on the task of picking his way down the hill. Something almost unprecedented was happening. He was having a good time! Independent of any conscious intent, joy percolated in his soul. The energizing pull of the valley sucked him downward, each careening step a challenge, each slip of his sandal a jolt of danger subdued. "The kingdom of heaven is like a lurching, almost-out-of-control tumble down a rugged hill." The thought tumbled through his mind and was gone, leaving only a wispy residue of recognition lost in a whirl of physical choices.

Bouncing and sliding, struggling to keep up with his feet, he careened past Mary, knowing a safe landing was waiting on the grassy bank of Brook Kidron but now caught up in what was almost airborne flight, exhilarated beyond reason, beyond common sense, beyond self-preservation. He was certain to fall, certain to break a leg, certain to skid face-down across the intoxicating patches of Shikaron or tendrils of Thorny Caper that dotted the hillside, certain to crash fatally into the trunk of a date palm. At the same time, it was certain that he would not do any of those things. He was not at the mercy of the hill; he *was* the hill. The energy of the hill was *his* energy. The character of the hill—the dead who lay in the hill's bosom, the ancient victors and vanquished who had trod the hill's blistered surface, the sun-blackened blood of countless sacrificial animals that caked the hill's slopes to the south—lifted him above the dance of his flailing feet, flowed over and under the span of his outstretched wings, wafted the spirit that was the Son of Man on currents that enabled him to swoop and glide and hover…and landed him gently on the green, knee-high grass that lined the banks of Brook Kidron.

Out of breath, still mentally soaring in ecstatic flight, Jesus gazed at the almost-dry creek bed before him. It was easy to envision the rushing flood of muddy water that would briefly fill the brook bank-to-bank during the winter rains. It was refreshing—reassuring—to mentally splash and luxuriate in the eternal coolness of the caves and tunnels of the Spring of Gihon that received and stored and surged this water of life into the City of David. Somehow it was good to imagine the swirling excess of a winter rain churning to the south as the brook rushed to join the lifeless water of the Dead Sea.

But now the brook seemed dry. The steady flow that oozed relentlessly southward beneath the stream bed slid silently, serenely, indiscernibly. "The kingdom of heaven is like an underground river, quietly filling the caverns of one's soul." Was that possible? Soaring majestically one minute; melodiously permeating the spirit of our being the next?

He turned and looked back at Mary and Nathanael as they picked their way down the slope, now almost at the bottom. Then he directed his attention once again to the waterless brook, surveyed with quiet eyes the road to Bethany and the groves of trees on the up-slope of the Mount of Olives beyond, and then sat down in the grass, listening to the swish of their feet moving through the grass, hearing the tone of their voices but not able to distinguish the words. He luxuriated in their nearness, basked in the anticipation of their touch.

He felt her standing next to him. "What was that all about?" she asked, her voice surrounding him as though from the clouds. A flash of memory intervened—the purity of a silent pool, warm sun on his back, a voice from somewhere outside the moment: "Repent, for the kingdom of heaven is at hand!"

Mary dropped down at his side and pushed her shoulder into his. "What was that all about?" she asked again.

He looked at her, felt his expression soften, then up at Nathanael, who was standing, his face set in an enigmatic smile. "Sit down next to me," Jesus said. He turned his head to indicate a spot on his left, sensing the moment fulfilled as Nathanael moved to the spot and settled down there, shoulder to shoulder, the three of them now living a connectedness that could not be explained.

For some time—Jesus had no idea for how long—they existed silently, alone in the kingdom. "What did you say to the priest at the Sheep Gate?" he asked finally.

She moved against his shoulder but said nothing.

"You aren't going to tell me?" he asked.

"*You* didn't answer *my* question," she replied. "Why should I answer yours?"

Had she asked a question? "What did you ask?"

"What was that all about?" she repeated.

He thought about how to answer. Somehow, trying to explain it would diminish the experience, yet she deserved an answer. If anyone would understand it, it would be Mary. "The kingdom of heaven is like a lurching, almost-out-of-control tumble down a rugged hill," he said, attempting to put into words what had existed as an inaccessible concept, as a Truth that could exist only outside of words.

She seemed to consider his explanation.

The brook and the grass and the presence of the hill recovered the moment. The coursing life shared through touching shoulders expanded and enveloped them.

Not an interruption but an augmentation, Mary's voice vibrated as part of their oneness. "I asked him a question," she said.

Jesus waited. He could feel Nathanael waiting as well.

"I asked him what the sheep's name was," she added finally.

Jesus looked sideways to his left, his eyes meeting Nathanael's eyes. At first the laughter was just a shared glint, almost imperceptible. "What the sheep's name was," he repeated, still locked into Nathanael's being.

He felt her nodding. The nod said that the sheep should have had a name, that every creature deserves the dignity of a name.

Nathanael's explosive snort set them off.

Jesus felt the laughter rumbling upward from his stomach, welcomed it and released it in a sort of rolling chortle that expanded into a steady, rhythmic guffaw.

Nathanael's snort became a choking, intermittent roar. He leaned into Jesus, pushing Jesus into Mary so that he fell into her lap.

Trying to catch his breath, Jesus looked up at Mary's face, recognizing by her distorted expression of delicious agony that her laughter was trapped inside, escaping by means of a series of soundless gasps. He sat up, threw his arms around her shoulders, and pulled her down with him into the grass.

Chest to chest she lay on top of him in a lightlessness that was not darkness, in a heaving, breathless, exultant oneness that was suddenly not laughter at all.

Still chest to chest, his arms still wrapped around her, they rolled onto their sides, sucking in air in gasps...transported, knowing, grieving.

19

His starved muscles respond without direction to his body's determination to survive: shoulders strain to pull him upward, knees straighten against the nails in his heels, lungs blow, shoulders release, knees unlock, rasping lungs suck air that does not fill, that does not nourish.

It was Simon. There was no doubt about that. The figure trudging up the hill from Bethany was still too far away to be seen clearly, but there was no mistaking that walk: head down, shoulders rolling in sync with each labored step. Simon was a man of the sea. On a boat, even in rough weather with the deck yawing and pitching, Simon moved with the grace and agility of a cat. On land, he was a plodder. Did that make sense? Either a man was lithe and supple or he was not. That being so, Simon's heavy, hulking pace must have nothing to do with his physical grace or lack of it. Simon's heart was on the sea. It was his heart, not his foot, that was heavy.

Jesus squatted next to the small pile of dry grass that he'd arranged on the ground, absently struck flint against pyrite to create a spark, and watched as a whiff of smoke and a spreading black burn announced the spark's success. There was always a quiet satisfaction that accompanied this process, a reassuring faith that there was an order and a significance to life on earth. If a man paid attention to the natural laws and lived his life within these limits—within this infinitude—he could be at peace with himself and with God.

He carefully sprinkled wood chips on the now-flickering tinder grass, thinking about Simon coming up the road, listening to the idle chatter of the men and women—his disciples, his friends—nearby, remembering the last time he'd been in this open area at the bank of the Brook Kidron. This afternoon there were still rivulets and pools remaining from the winter rains. It was a good place to set up camp, a good place to use as their home base during the seven days of Passover.

Could it really be six months since he and Mary and Nathanael had rolled deliciously in the grass and laughed to the point of breathlessness in this very spot? Six months of teaching in Galilee. Six months of frustration and discouragement. Did anyone really understand? Had any of the thousands of people they'd talked to during that time found their way into the kingdom of heaven? It was all well and good to generate enthusiasm and excitement among the marginal people of Israel, but how long could the energy last? How long before every one of those people was consumed once again by the pain and seeming pointlessness of the daily struggle to survive within the domination of the kingdom of man?

Carefully he placed three small sticks so that they formed a triangle over the gently spreading flame consuming the wood chips. For a brief time he studied the patient tongues of fire as they flicked upward to touch the sticks, to draw life from them, to become the sticks.

He added sticks, waited, added larger sticks. Finally he settled back into a sitting position, wrapping his arms around his knees and focusing on the fire, on the memories within the fire.

"It's absolutely crazy!" Mary had argued. "You must have a death wish." They'd been coming down the hill near Bethsaida, a few hangers-on from that afternoon's gathering following at a distance, but, for the most part, they'd been alone.

He hadn't replied. After all, what was there to say that might persuade her that a return to Jerusalem for Passover was a good idea? The Romans saw him as a rabble rouser, another in a long line of messianic pretenders who stirred up trouble. The Temple priests saw him as a threat to their control over the people. Who knew? Maybe some of them honestly believed that Jesus' heretical teachings would bring the wrath of God down upon them. Whatever any of them actually believed, the fact was that they all would be pleased to eliminate him.

"They know who you are," Mary had continued. "They know what you look like. They'll know how to find you in Jerusalem."

He was walking faster now, eager to get back to Capernaum, eager to relax with his friends in Simon's courtyard. Eager to enjoy a cup or two of wine.

Mary's voice had became a little breathless as she hurried to keep up with him. "You don't have to be in Jerusalem to take your message to the people," she'd persisted. "The peasants in Galilee need you much more than the merchants and businessmen of the city do."

He stopped, at the same time putting his arms out to stop her. One outstretched arm now resting on each of her shoulders, he spoke to her with his eyes. "You're correct," his eyes said. "It's dangerous for me—for all of us—in Jerusalem. The kingdom of heaven is available in the countryside just as it is in the city. If we stay where we are, we can probably live a long and happy life."

She had turned her head away, not wanting to listen to his eyes.

"I have to go to Jerusalem," he'd said to the side of her face, his voice almost a whisper. "I don't know why." It would have been pretentious to reason that it was God's will, that this was part of a cosmic scheme over which they had no control.

She turned her head back to speak with her own glistening eyes. A tear slid down her cheek. Wiping it away with the back of her hand, she shifted her gaze so that she was staring past him, over his shoulder, as though the mountains behind him might provide answers, as though the secret to understanding him might be written in the gathering gloom of the eastern sky. Finally, she looked at his hand on her shoulder, wrapped both her hands around that hand, and managed a thin smile.

Her words repeated themselves over and over in Jesus' memory now as the image of her face lingered in the flames of the fire. "I guess we're going to Jerusalem," she had said. That had been it. "I guess we're going to Jerusalem."

"By tomorrow night that fire will be just right for roasting a lamb."

Jesus, startled, looked up. James was standing at his side.

"Preparation Day began at sunset," James said. "Passover Dinner is tomorrow night."

He placed some wood on the fire and sat down next to Jesus. "Gotta have lamb," he added, almost to himself.

Jesus smiled. Mary had disappeared from the flames, but he continued to stare at the emptiness. It was always difficult to know what James was thinking. There was no lamb. There would be no lamb. James should know that, yet the tone of his comments wasn't the tone of irony. They had come to Jerusalem for Passover as God required, his manner suggested. The lamb would be part of the deal. "Do you come to Jerusalem every year for Passover?" Jesus asked.

James grunted negatively.

"Ever?"

Another grunt. He had never been to Jerusalem for Passover.

"In Galilee, then," Jesus persisted. "Every year your father's household sacrifices a lamb?"

"Jerusalem is the place the Lord God has chosen," James said to the flames. A brief silence followed before he added, "What would be the point in sacrificing a lamb in Galilee?"

Jesus didn't answer. What would be the point in sacrificing a lamb anywhere? The story of Moses and the Israelites being brought out of Egypt was a good one, but the God Jesus knew would not have been interested in killing the first-born. What kind of a God would harden Pharaoh's heart and then punish Pharaoh with horrible plagues for having a hard heart?

"Do you?" James asked.

"Do I what?" Jesus asked.

"Come to Jerusalem every year for Passover."

Jesus shook his head. "This is the first time," he said, feeling guilty in spite of his conviction that God had had nothing to do with the naming of the city as the only place where sacrifices could be made. "It's a rich man's journey," he added. "My family never owned a sheep, blemished or unblemished." The image of four rows of rings in the Court of the Priests, each ring holding a struggling, bleating sheep, gathered in his mind. The flowing, blood-streaked water swirled before him. On the hill behind him, beyond the heavy stones of the east wall, beneath the golden roof of the Temple glittering in the late light of the setting sun, the slaughter was going on at this very moment.

Simon climbed the bank of the brook and joined them at the fire, dropping a sack next to James and giving John, who had sat down while Jesus was speaking, a push in the behind with his foot. He was breathing heavily. "They're all thieves," he grumbled. "You wouldn't believe what they charged me for a few dried fish and some loaves of bread."

"Unleavened?" John asked.

"Of course not unleavened," Simon answered. "Have you ever tasted unleavened bread?" He plopped himself heavily next to John.

"The feast begins tomorrow," James intervened. "Unleavened bread, an unblemished male lamb..." He looked past his brother at Simon's glowering face. "...the lamb's blood on the doorposts, the Angel of Death swooping soundlessly through the sky."

Simon looked tiredly across the fire at Jesus. "Do we really have to put up with this nonsense?" the look asked silently. "I've just spent most of my money for some bread and fish that may last us a couple of days."

"James," Jesus said, "the Angel of Death will not be swooping overhead." Even as he spoke the words, a shiver, like an icy flash of lightning, crackled the length of his spine.

For a while, no one spoke.

"Personally," John said after more of the disciples had joined them around the fire, "I don't care for lamb. There's nothing like smoked fish." He leaned heavily against Simon's shoulder. "And bread...leavened bread...and wine."

Jesus watched as the circle of people grew larger. It was no longer just the disciples. There were a dozen or more people, people he didn't recognize, standing in the shadowy perimeter of the group. He felt Mary settle down next to him, took in the essence of her, experienced the peace that she exuded, accepted the cup that she handed him and watched her hands as she poured wine from a wineskin into the cup. Then he watched in silence, unusually at peace in the moment, as the skin was passed from disciple to disciple, as cups were filled, as gentle, seemingly self-conscious comments were exchanged. Each cup, each pair of callused hands, each pair of sun-lined eyes, each pair of dry, impatient lips were the focus of his own probing vision.

When Simon's cup was filled, Jesus motioned with his hand toward the sack of food that the big man had brought from Bethany. By means of a series of gestures and nods, he was able to get a loaf of bread passed from hand to hand until it reached him. Grasping his cup in one hand and the bread in the other, he feigned confusion, finally handing his cup to Mary so that she held her own cup along with his.

"This is the bread of life," he said, holding the loaf in both hands and extending his arms toward the center of the group. What, exactly, did he want to say? No, that wasn't the question that was bothering him. He knew what he wanted to say. The problem was that he didn't know how to say it. What words could he string together that would clearly make the point that had to be made?

He was in the wilderness again. "If you are the Son of God," the Adversary was saying to him, "tell this stone to become bread." His response had come easily, so easily that it had not seemed to come from him at all. "Man shall not live on bread alone," he had said.

"But man shall not live on bread alone," he said again, this time into the undulating light and gathering darkness of this Preparation Day night.

The listeners waited in silence. Overhead, a full moon seemed to have halted its journey to hang directly overhead and illuminate the night.

Jesus looked from fire-reflecting face to fire-reflecting face: Simon, John, James, Salome, Nathanael, Perpetua, Andrew, Philip; he looked past them toward the unknown faces beyond. "It's appropriate on this first night of Passover to consider the Israelites," he said. "Their story teaches us much about God."

"Forty years in the wilderness," called an unfamiliar voice from beyond the fire's reach.

Jesus nodded, distracted but determined not to allow himself to be sidetracked. He wanted to talk about bread—about the lack of bread. "The story tells us that the people had nothing to eat," he continued.

"The Lord sent quail."

This time Jesus recognized Simon's voice. "The Scriptures tell us that," he said. This was not going well. He didn't want to talk about quail. "I don't know if it happened that way or not," he added. "It's a story." Should he have said that? Did that fact somehow diminish the story's truth? "Moses tells us," he continued, "that in the evening quail covered the camp. And the next morning, when the dew had evaporated, the ground was covered with a strange flake-like substance."

Several voices spoke the word. "Manna." It was like telling a well-loved tale to a bunch of kids.

"Bread." It was Simon's voice.

"Yes and no," Jesus said. He held up the loaf of bread again. "It wasn't this. We shouldn't picture loaves of bread crashing to the ground."

Someone far in the back made a comment that led to other joking remarks and general laughter.

"I'm going to call it bread," Jesus said, now speaking more loudly to regain the attention of the group. "It was the bread of life, but it was not bread at all. God didn't *send* the Manna. Actually, there were no flakes on the ground, no white seeds like coriander. God didn't send anything that the people didn't already have. God *was* the Manna—*is* the Manna."

He paused, waiting for a reaction that did not come. Either they had not heard, or they had not understood. This was so difficult! Where were the words he needed? "We must not," he began again, "we must not picture God in the sky looking down upon the Israelites and sending them bread as a sign that he would take care of them."

Okay. What we must *not* do was the easy part. The hard part was what we *must* do instead.

He plunged ahead. "Picture each man waking up in the morning on the Sinai with the revelation that he is a manifestation of God, that God is heaven and earth and every living thing in heaven and earth.

Once each man comes to this realization, he *knows*—he is ecstatic. He need not fear anything. *He need not fear anything!* He understands that his existence will be as it must be. He will survive or die in the wilderness. He will contribute to life as it is his nature to contribute."

Jesus' frustration mounted. It was always easy to know when your audience was with you, always exciting to feed on the energy that flowed between teacher and students. It was always easy, as well, to know when you were alone. Right now, he was all by himself.

"Manna was the storyteller's way of describing this revelation," he added futilely.

You knew you were in trouble when you had to start explaining.

"Manna—bread—is the symbol of life within God. Every human being who knows God in this way will be at peace with himself."

"For forty years?"

This time it was Nathanael. Jesus looked in the direction of the voice, made eye contact, and smiled. "For forty lifetimes," he said. "Four times forty lifetimes."

"Four hundred times forty lifetimes," Simon added.

Jesus held the loaf in the air again, this time with one hand. "This is the bread of life," he repeated. "It is the symbol of man's life within God."

"And woman's," Mary interjected.

He looked at her, shifted the loaf of bread to his left hand, and put his right arm around her shoulders. "And woman's," he shouted.

20

Her face...again, her face...mouth set in amusement beneath dancing eyes.

Jesus wills a stagnant mind to bear on the image, to examine it, to hang on to the joy of it, to expand the face and re-experience it. They sit beside the road. Mary teases him; he is defensive, loving her challenge yet fearing the certainty of her knowing. What has he done—or not done? The cross won't allow him to remember.

"Go away!" It is the desperate screech of an old woman. "God gave me fingers that won't bend! Who are you to heal them?"

Who is he, indeed? Mary's eyes know. They will always know. Even now, as horrible muscle cramps twist his legs into rigid knots and fiery internal flames consume his internal organs, Mary's optic smile comforts him, consoles him, reassures him.

James had added more wood to the fire so that the flames blazed brightly in the darkness of the Kidron Valley, but the laughter and cheers and suggestive comments had died down. For a while the fire's crackle was the only sound.

"But what does it mean?" Andrew's voice lay soft and pensive on the damp night air.

Jesus looked in the direction of the voice but could not pick Andrew out of the shadows. "What does *what* mean?" he asked.

"For me to have peace, I have to know God." The voice from the darkness seemed almost like a whisper from God.

Jesus nodded.

"What does it mean to know God?

So, that's what it all came down to, didn't it. It was all very well to serve nice-sounding phrases for the people to chew on, but of what value was any idea that they couldn't digest? Could any human being actually know God? Explain God? Understand God?

"Andrew," Jesus began, still not sure of what he was going to say, "Andrew, each of us is different." Was that true? How many people were there on earth? Was it possible that each person was one of a kind? Yes, he decided, it had to be true.

Voices in the distance penetrated the bubble of soundlessness that enclosed the group around the fire. People moving along the road toward Bethany? People in Gethsemane beyond the road?

"Are you and your brother Simon a lot alike?

Simon snorted his amusement at the suggestion. John leaned toward him and made what was probably a sarcastic comment.

"Each of you has his own nature, his own way of thinking, his own way of dealing with problems, his own way of doing almost everything." He came out of the thought, recognizing that the point he was attempting to make was eluding him. Staring downward at the loaf of bread in his hands, he realized that Mary was still holding his cup of wine. He turned his head to smile at her, took his cup from her hand, and replaced it with the loaf of bread. Lifting the cup and moving it slowly so that he had acknowledged every person gathered around him, he said, "God is this cup of wine."

Soundlessness! Jesus' words hung in the surreal dance of the fire. At this moment, life on earth seemed limited to this pinpoint of light in the darkness of all existence.

"God is not an angry father in the sky," Jesus continued. "*You* are God."

No one spoke. No one moved. No one breathed. Each person, rather, seemed to share a collective breath that was the breath of God—the breath of all humankind.

"*I* am God." Jesus heard the thought, embraced it, but knew it would be misunderstood. He raised his head and gazed at the now silver moon. It was like being in a long dark tunnel and seeing light in the distance that was the end of the tunnel. "The moon is God," he heard himself say. "This brook, flowing deep underground into the Spring of Gihon, is God." He hesitated, knowing that what he was about to say would take his listeners to a place they would not want to go. "Herod the Great was God," he added. "Pontius Pilate is God."

The listeners were stirring now. A restless discomfort had settled over them.

"Andrew," he continued, "you were brought into this world for a reason. If you are true to what you are—to who you are—then you are *knowing* God."

"Pontius Pilate is a murderer." The thought was spoken sullenly from the front row of those seated on the other side of the fire. It was Nathanael's thought.

Jesus nodded. "The kingdom of heaven needs murderers," he said. "The kingdom of heaven needs victims of murderers." It was a frightening thought! An impossible thought! What about 'love your enemy'? What about doing unto others as you would have them do unto you? How was it possible that he was sitting here now contradicting the very heart of what he'd been teaching for the past year?

Philip, strangely subdued up to this point, now spoke up. "You shall not murder," he argued.

A general murmur of agreement arose tentatively from the crowd.

Jesus drank from his cup before replying. "You shall not commit adultery," he began. "You shall not steal. You shall not bear false witness. You shall not covet your neighbor's possessions." He was stalling. If this moment with his friends was an epiphany, he had to open his mind and soul; he had to trust that God would get it right. And...this was the terrible possibility that made him hesitate...and if this was not God but his own fallible brain that was conjuring up demons, he had to shake himself loose from the doubt-induced untruths.

Philip had punctuated each commandment with a firm "Yes."

"And yet the Scriptures are filled with stories of murder and theft and lying and coveting," Jesus continued, "often in the name of God." He heard his voice rising but had no desire to tone it down. He was certain now. God was speaking! "Israelite armies slaughtered and pillaged and raped the Midianites, Edomites, Moabites, and Ammonites before crossing the Jordan into Canaan. For over a thousand years since that time, the rulers of Israel—yes, even the beloved King David—have regularly broken every law in the Books of Moses."

He took another sip of wine and waited for a reaction, exhilarated by the words he was hearing himself speak, by the convictions that he hadn't known he held.

For some reason, there was no immediate response to his outburst. It was as though the crowd had accepted Philip as its spokesman and was waiting for him to continue.

"Breaking the Law doesn't make it right," Philip said at last. "Sin is sin, whether you're a king or a priest or a tax collector." He scanned the circle until he found Mathew, grinning an apology and giving the tax gatherer an abbreviated salute.

"Philip," Jesus began, "we're talking about two different things." He shifted his position in an effort to ease a stiffness that was settling in his back. He'd been seated on the cold ground for a long time. "I'm talking about God. You're talking about the laws of man. Men have to make laws so that they can live together in limited conflict. Laws are intended to control those who would take advantage of their neighbor. Laws use punishment or the threat of punishment to deter people from causing problems for others."

Philip tried to break in, but Jesus held up his hand to stop him.

"God is not about laws," Jesus continued. "God is not about sin and punishment. God is not a meta-person who thinks like human beings or has human needs. God does not exist *somewhere*. God *Is*!"

Philip was silently staring into the fire. James, perhaps dreaming of roasted lamb, gazed at the ground. Simon was studying his left hand, massaging the fingers of that hand as though there was a pain that he might eliminate through abuse. Around the circle, no one seemed willing to meet Jesus' gaze.

"Your job is to be true to your nature, to contribute to life that miniscule gift that you alone can give. It's the same for me—for everyone. When we accomplish this, we are at peace. We are in the kingdom of heaven." He raised his almost empty cup into the air and directed it toward those around the circle. "Mazel Tov," he said.

21

A raging thirst ravages him, sucking the essence of his Self from the decimated shell that is his body. It is as though dry, brittle shards of his vital organs are crumbling and swirling in a great dust cloud that blackens the sky of his being. His shriveled tongue would caress blistered lips but lies burnt and inert in a barren mouth.

There is no conscious thought of breathing, but involuntarily the cramped muscles in his burning shoulders contract and pull his body upward. A rasping cough burns his withered lungs.

"I still don't get it," Andrew grumbled. His tone was not argumentative. He was not implying that Jesus' explanation had been faulty. Instead, it was a tone of self-deprecation. He did not get it because he was lacking the capacity to understand any but the most obvious of truths.

The upper branches of the olive trees on this side of the Kidron were eerily silhouetted against the brightness of the full moon. On the upslope beneath the trees, Gethsemene was shadowed and distorted to the eye. Not far to the west, on the other side of the road and the brook, the fire had no doubt dwindled to glowing coals. The warmth of that fire would have been welcome right now.

"What don't you get?" Jesus asked as the three of them moved carefully in single file through the darkness, Nathanael leading the way.

Andrew's thin frame seemed to slump in disappointment as Jesus studied him from the end of the short line. "Well," Andrew began, the rhythm of his words slow and reaching in cadence with his stride, "if I am God and you are God and Herod the Great was God and..." Several strides filled a lengthy interval. "...if everyone is God..."

Jesus knew the question that was coming but waited for Andrew to put it together for himself.

"...if everyone is God, what about good and evil?"

"What about it?" Jesus asked.

Nathanael stopped and turned around to take part in the discussion, causing Andrew to bump into him. "God is good," Nathanael said. "Herod was evil."

"Exactly," Andrew enthused.

Jesus took a deep breath, sensing rather than seeing the intense expression on the faces of the two men, wanting desperately to clarify a concept that was difficult even for him. "What does it mean to be good?" he asked. It sounded like a dumb question, but the answer was at the heart of the matter.

A long silence seemed to be a part of the darkness. "Honesty," Nathanael answered.

"Kindness," Andrew added. "Concern for others."

Fairness. Friendliness. Trustworthiness. Being dependable. Hard work. Generosity. Love. Their listing gained momentum.

"Bravery?" Jesus interrupted.

There was a pause, as though the two men suspected a trick question. "Yes," they answered in unison.

"Cannibalism?"

"Cannibalism?"

"Eating human flesh."

Nathanael made a gagging sound.

"Of course not," Andrew answered.

"How about animal sacrifice?"

Neither man answered.

"Human sacrifice?"

Again no answer. They were onto him now, wary, recognizing that they were being set up.

Jesus moved to his right through the darkness, hoping to find a level spot where they could sit down. Finding only a steeper slope and dense growth that he couldn't identify, he returned to the trail. "Let's walk a little further and find a place to sit down," he said.

"We could go back to where we left Simon and the others," Andrew suggested.

"No, we'll find something," Jesus said. He didn't want to deal with a group right now. Actually, he wanted to be left alone for a while. An ominous pall more dense than the physical gloom of this Gethsemene night had settled over his spirit in recent days. He wanted to get *inside* himself. He wanted to get *outside* himself. Somehow it seemed that this discussion might help him break through the gloom of his soul. Strangely, Nathanael and Andrew were making it possible for him to satiate his hunger for aloneness.

They moved further up the trail, good and evil stalking their every step.

Nathanael stopped. They had moved temporarily beyond the trees so that the area was bathed in moonlight. Obviously others had stopped here before—many others, many times. There was the trunk of a felled olive tree to sit on. Jesus sat, not because he was tired but because he was focused—Nathanael on his right, Andrew on his left.

"There have been people throughout the centuries," he began, "who have eaten human flesh. In these cultures, it was believed that God saw this practice as holy and good."

Nathanael moved restlessly.

"There have been cultures—right here in the land that we now consider Israel—that sacrificed children to El, to Baal, to Asherah."

"They thought it was good," Andrew said, his voice low, almost confidential.

"They thought it was good," Jesus repeated. He paused, not for effect but to ponder what he wanted to say next. "For as long as there have been humans on earth—I have no idea the period of time that represents…"

"A long time," Andrew volunteered.

"For as long as there have been humans on earth," Jesus repeated, "people have been trying to define who they are and why they are. Always their explanations have been limited by their minds. Always the explanations were based on what the human mind could understand, on what the human mind could imagine. They concluded that there must be powers greater than themselves—gods. Human minds imagined gods. The gods they imagined—created—were invariably very much like themselves."

"That's what we're doing right now." Nathanael's voice rumbled in the chill air, an early morning voice that seemed to resonate in depths within great depths. "The God we create tells us what is good and what is bad."

The next question hung unacknowledged in the damp air, too fearful to be asked, too crucial to be ignored.

"Then God doesn't really exist?" Andrew's tone almost seemed to be one of relief.

"God exists!" Nathanael's response was probably directed more to himself than to Andrew, more to God than to himself.

Jesus was content to be silent in the moment, to be as one with Nathanael, to bask in the energy of Nathanael's triumph.

"Good and evil do not exist," Nathanael continued. "Everything is God. God cannot be complete if the thieves and murderers of the earth are not a part of him."

"But…"

Jesus turned his head and watched the questions race across the surface of Andrew's moonlit face like a line of ocean swells on a stormy sea. Then he twisted to look over the other shoulder at Nathanael and exchange a tight smile.

"But what's the point…" Andrew began at last, directing his words into the night, "what's the point in being honest or trustworthy or kind or…any of those things we said are good?"

Jesus said nothing. Transported beyond the moment, beyond the awareness that was himself, he became everything and nothing: *the muffled beat of powerful owl wings, the soundless swoop in the cavernous blackness that was the light of night, the death squeal of a talon-pierced rabbit; the darting gray flash of a constrictor, the breathless, eye popping gasp of a stiff-tailed mouse; the flowing sinew of a lion in pursuit, the terror-filled flight of a zebra herd, the strength of crushing jaws breaking the neck of a fallen straggler. Warm, pulsing life. Living, endless death. Light—expanding, retreating, enveloping, piercing.*

"…forever."

What had Andrew said? Only the final word registered in Jesus' consciousness. Forever. What a strange word! Forever. What could it possibly mean? "I'm sorry, Andrew," he said. *Wings spread in silent descent. Talons extend. Shriek!* "I wasn't paying attention."

"You promised us the kingdom of heaven. You said we would live forever."

"That's still my promise, Andrew."

"But we don't have to be good."

"Yes, we do." Should he explain it again?

Nathanael spared him that task. "Each of us has to be true to what our nature defines as good."

Jesus leaned into him so that they bumped shoulders, a connection in spirit that required no words.

For a while in the moonlit darkness, they sat without speaking.

"And..."

Jesus tensed as Andrew broke the silence.

"...Herod and I will both go...will both find peace in the kingdom of heaven, he for causing endless suffering and I for loving my enemy."

Jesus looked at Andrew and grinned. "I don't know about you and Herod," he said. "I really don't know. I can be sure only of what brings peace to me."

"Forever!" Andrew was sitting up straight, his hands on his knees, smiling. "Forever and ever," he repeated.

"Whatever that means," Nathanael scoffed. "Maybe 'forever' just means until you die."

"Maybe it does," Jesus agreed. His mind toyed with the concept. Could 'forever' possibly be measured by the passing of time? Could the Creator of Heaven and Earth be concerned about days and months and years? He pictured God sitting on his throne in heaven. On the wall to God's right a huge calendar keeps track of the years since the Creation, a big X canceling each completed year. There are 3,793 Xs.

22

A steady, single-pitched groan penetrates the burning fog that is Jesus' consciousness. It is his groan, spontaneous, the product of some deep part of him over which he has no control. At the same time, his sluggish brain reasons, it is the groan of all humankind. He wonders about Mary—if she hears.

Voices! At first, faint, distant voices, heard only in a deep, unacknowledged awareness. It was not until an angry shout reverberated through the Gethsemene moon shadows that the earlier voices broke into Jesus' consciousness.

"Simon!" Andrew said.

Jesus stared into the tangle of olive tree branches silhouetted against the silver luminescence of the moon. He shivered, sensing the silent spread of wings overhead.

Nathanael stood up, seeming to hover protectively for what must have been only seconds but what felt like an eternity. Together, the three of them listened with a sense of hearing intensified to the point of being painful.

Below them, where they had left Simon, James, and John, men were arguing. Jesus imagined torches held high in the hands of Roman soldiers, shadows undulating ominously, angry, glistening sweat on sun-worn faces.

"They can't catch up with us," Nathanael said. "We can find our way over the mountain and down into the Jordan Valley."

Andrew was standing now, as well, but saying nothing. Jesus felt his terror, heard his unspoken plea for mercy, knew the profession of innocence that was already forming on his lips.

"We can cross the river and be heading north through Perea by sunrise," Nathanael said.

Jesus played out their escape in his mind. Nathanael was correct. In a few days they would be back in Galilee. Simon and the others would follow. The Romans wanted Jesus the rabble rouser, not his disciples. If the leader was arrested and crucified, the movement would disintegrate.

"Let's go!" Andrew said. "Simon will be okay. They'll all be okay."

Jesus could not distinguish the words that were being spoken below, but he could imagine what was being said. Simon would be claiming that he didn't know the man. James and John would be supporting the story. They had innocently stopped by to listen to the man's ravings around the fire earlier that night. They were poor tenants working the land north of Jerusalem and had come to the city to have a good time during Passover. There was no doubt about it. Simon would talk his way out of the situation.

Nathanael moved so that he stood in front of Jesus. Not speaking, he gazed downward until Jesus raised his head and their eyes met. Nathanael held out one hand. Jesus took it with both of his own and allowed Nathanael to pull him to his feet. "We can wait for Simon and the others in Bethany beyond the Jordan," Nathanael said.

Was it really to end this way? Running? Hiding? Settling down anonymously somewhere in the north? Had he done all that he could do? Was the kingdom of heaven waiting for him in Galilee? Had he come to Jerusalem at Passover only to run for home at the first sign of danger?

Andrew was moving behind him, probably taking a few steps up the trail. In front of him, Nathanael crossed his arms and assumed a stance that was eloquent in its silence. "What are you thinking?" the stance said. "How can you be considering any action other than getting the heck out of here?"

Certainly it had nothing to do with bravery. Maybe it was quite the opposite. Maybe he was frozen with fear. Maybe he was being irrational. Was he responding to the part of him that was weak and human or to the part of him that was God? Was it his role to die for the message he'd brought to humankind? Was it his role to live and continue teaching the good news to others? And who was to say that this was a life-threatening situation? Who was to say that the voices in the distance were the voices of Roman soldiers? And, if it was indeed soldiers, who was to say that they represented a threat?

"You two wait here," he said. "I'll go down and find out what's going on."

"Teacher," Nathanael replied, "nothing good is going to happen if you go back down the hill."

"They'll arrest you," Andrew said.

Jesus turned his head to look at Andrew and then shifted his gaze in the direction of the path leading downward. "Maybe," he said. And if they arrested him? What then? A warning? Prison? His head, like John's, lopped off and presented as a gift? To whom? What would such a death be like? Quick? Clean? Would he shriek like the rabbit?

"They'll crucify you," Nathanael said.

Crucifixion! He'd seen the crosses outside the city's walls. He'd seen the decaying bodies. He'd smelled the intolerable stench. That's what the Romans did to troublemakers. It had been Herod Antipas, not the Romans, who had given John the gift of painless death. Pontius Pilate would be interested, not in killing Jesus, but in prolonging his agonizing death, in providing an example to deter others who might speak of freedom. Pilate was not the owl, the constrictor, the lion. Pilate was human. Pilate had no interest in death. Pilate dealt in lingering pain and humiliation. No one, not for any reason, should have to die on the cross. What possible good could come from such a sacrifice?

Jesus turned again to look at Andrew and the darkness beyond that would lead them to safety. It was time to retreat. They could continue teaching in Galilee. He was of no use to the people if he were hanging on a tree. "Let's get out of here," he said.

Andrew nodded, turned, and started up the trail. Jesus followed, feeling Nathanael take up a position behind him as they moved out of the moonlight and into denser growth.

There really was no trail now. Andrew was picking his way slowly along the side of the hill, probably trying to envision the mountain and work his way around it rather than over it. After a few minutes, he stopped. "I don't know where I'm going," he said. "Let's let Nathanael lead the way."

"Just try to stay at this same level," Nathanael said. "Don't go higher or lower. Eventually we'll break into the clear and then head down onto the road."

Jesus sat down, lifted himself slightly to move away from something sharp beneath him, and settled down again, gazing into the gloom. A chill raced up his spine and radiated in all directions across his back He shivered. From the depth of his being, despair welled up and inundated what must be his soul. His eyes stung with tears. He willed his mind to control whatever this was that was happening to him, but the mind, swollen, immobilized by an expanding, throbbing, internal pressure, could not acknowledge his command.

Nathanael's voice seemed to come from a great distance. "Teacher," he asked, "are you okay?"

Jesus heard the question, understood it abstractly, but could not form a response. Instead, he closed his eyes tightly and allowed his being to exist in its own place, in its own time, a drifting, shifting kaleidoscope of sense and nonsense for which he was nothing more than the vessel.

Gradually, almost imperceptibly, the pieces fell into place. The throbbing settled into a series of pulsating tones and eventually into a warm sense of bubbling contentment. The radiating chills became a refreshing coolness. The rising flood of despair slowed, lapped harmlessly against his emotional dykes, and receded until it became a rippling stream replenishing a crystal sylvan pond. Salt-stiffened eyes still shut tightly, Jesus took a deep breath and allowed his mind to luxuriate in a pervasive inner peace. His breathing became slow and regular. In spite of the perspiration-soaked tunic that clung to his back, he felt warm, secure and warm, like a fetus in a womb, passively receptive to the voices of the earth. Gradually, however, the reality of the moment penetrated the protective barrier. He became aware again of the presence of Andrew to his right and Nathanael to his left, their concern palpable in the aura of this dark place on the slope of the Mount of Olives.

He opened his eyes and studied the faceless shape of Nathanael. "I've got to go back," he said. There was no sense of good or bad in the statement. It was a simple declaration, a calm acknowledgement of what had to be done. If he walked down that hill to meet the Palace Guard, no matter what might happen to him there or later, he would be at peace with God.

23

The awful pain is more than he can bear. He would scream, but there is no breath for screaming, no moisture in his parched body to allow even a gasping whisper. A silent prayer for death, once a courageous entreaty, now a pitiful whimper, repeats itself endlessly in his soul. Eyes clamped shut, head down, chin against chest, shoulders slumped, Jesus endures. There is no choice but to endure.

The glow from the torches ahead wavered eerily among the surrounding olive trees as the three of them reached the clearing and stopped to survey the scene. To their right was a small squad of soldiers wearing helmets and probably carrying short swords but not really in battle gear—no shields, no spears—dressed in some sort of armor that looked more decorative than functional. In front of this group, talking to Simon, James, and John, was the leader, more than likely not much higher in rank than the men he led. Obviously, whatever the squad's purpose, the soldiers did not see it as particularly important or dangerous. Their demeanor suggested the boredom of waiting rather than the energy of combat. The number of troops in the city was always increased significantly for the high holy days. For the most part, their objective was to be visible and keep the people in line rather than to do battle. It was not exciting work.

Jesus looked at Nathanael and raised his eyebrows, receiving a shrug of the shoulders in reply. He directed his attention again to the squad leader and attempted to pick up, not the words that were being spoken—they were too far away for that—but the timbre of the voices, the body language, of the four men involved. "I think we're okay," he said, almost to himself.

"There's only eight of them," Nathanael responded. "Only two more than us."

"We've got God on our side," Andrew said.

Jesus elbowed him gently in the ribs. "So do they," he said.

"I don't like it," Nathanael muttered.

Liking it was not the point. The situation was what it was. "Let's get it over with," Jesus answered, beginning to move toward the torches, hesitantly at first but then striding with what he hoped was authority. Almost immediately Nathanael was at his side and moving ahead, setting a pace that Jesus had difficulty matching. Jesus glanced over his shoulder to determine that Andrew was following but then focused his attention forward, riveting his gaze on what was going on ahead of him.

They were perhaps 40 strides from the group when Simon's body language changed. What was it? Something indefinable. A slump of the shoulders? A tilt of the head? A shifting of the feet? He had seen them coming. That was clear enough. He was not pleased to see them. That was even more clear.

The squad leader, whose back had been to the approaching trio, obviously picked up on Simon's discomfort. His shoulders seemed to stiffen, and he turned to look behind him. His action alerted his squad of milites, the foremost of whom drew his sword but let his arm hang at his side. He seemed alert but not alarmed, ready for a fight but not expecting one.

When the distance between them had narrowed to perhaps twenty paces, Jesus stopped. Nathanael took several more strides, stopped, looked over his shoulder questioningly, and then returned his attention to the group ahead of them. Andrew, when he'd caught up, stopped at Jesus' left. For what felt like a long period of time, the two groups stared at each other in silence.

"Is there something I can do for you, Centurion?" Jesus asked.

Nathanael turned and moved back toward Jesus. "He's not a Centurion," he said, his voice low and confidential.

"I know that," Jesus replied, matching Nathanael's confidential tone. "But what do I call him?"

"He's probably an Optio." Andrew didn't bother to lower his voice. "Or maybe a Tesserarius."

Jesus and Nathanael both turned to look at him, then at each other. Jesus read in Nathanael's expression exactly what he himself was wondering. How in the world would Andrew know what an Optio was…or a Tesserarius?

Whatever the man's title might be, the problem remained the same. What did one say to an officer of the Roman Empire? How did one say it? One took orders from such an individual. One did as he was told. He avoided confrontations. Nothing good could come from questioning—from resisting. Still, there was the matter of self-respect. There was the matter of one's relationship with himself.

"Are you Jesus, the king of the Jews?" the Optio asked.

Jesus' gaze shifted to Simon, their eyes meeting briefly before Simon looked away. "There is no king of the Jews," he answered. "There has been no king since Zedekiah, over 600 years ago."

The Optio took several steps toward him and stopped. "Are you the one they call 'the Messiah'?" he asked.

Jesus saw that this was a young man, a man who was carrying out orders, a man who was not interested in circumstances but in duty. "I don't call myself that," Jesus replied. "What others say is beyond my control." Behind the Optio, Simon was shaking his head and mouthing instructions. "Say no!" his lips said silently.

The Optio's facial expression made his annoyance clear enough. All of the milites had now drawn their swords. Nathanael took several steps toward them, stopping close to the Optio but facing the squad. Simon moved to within a few steps of the Optio. Beneath wild, desperate eyes, his lips shaped themselves into a new message: "Run!"

"You're going to have to come with us," the Optio said, not seeming intimidated by the approach of either man.

Jesus took a deep breath. He was going to have to go with them. Was there an alternative? He knew there was not. When he'd changed his mind up there on the hill, he'd known. Walking back down through the olive grove, he'd known. Maybe he'd always known. He was to be arrested like a common criminal. His crime? Loving his fellow man. "I've broken no laws," he said, realizing, even as the words formed, that this was not true. He'd broken no Roman laws. The laws of Moses? Well, why should Caesar care about that?

"It's not my job to judge you," the Optio said. "It's my job to arrest you. The Procurator will determine your guilt or innocence." He looked over his shoulder and motioned for his milites to move forward.

"Run, Teacher!" Simon roared before crashing into the back of the Optio, knocking the man to the ground and falling on top of him.

In the seconds—in the surreal, shadowed eternity—that followed, Jesus stood in frozen horror as chaos erupted around him. James and John rushed to assist Simon, James wresting the Optio's sword from its scabbard and turning to face the milites, who were moving, not in a wild attack but in a controlled advance, their swords drawn and ready. John, his own knife in his hand, dropped to his knees next to the

Optio's head and held the knife to the leader's throat, saying nothing but making it clear that the Optio's jugular would be slashed if the troops came near.

Nathanael, obviously surprised by Simon's attack, hesitated, seeing the two men crash to the ground but making no move to help. Switching his attention to the milites, he watched them only briefly before looking back at the fallen Optio, who was immobilized under the weight and strength of the big fisherman. Then a quick look back at Jesus, their eyes meeting in a flicker of understanding that was a lifetime. "For God's sake!" he screamed. "Run!"

Jesus was only vaguely aware of Andrew's hands grabbing his arm, pulling it, of Andrew's pleading voice. "Teacher!" he entreated. "We can get back up the hill!"

Through a blur of burning tears, Jesus watched: Simon like an angry bear atop a motionless Optio; John, his knife at the man's throat; James, suddenly a warrior, poised over the men on the ground, a sword extended threateningly toward the approaching Roman squad; the soldiers advancing with a deliberate, military precision that spoke of hundreds of years of perfecting the skills of violence and death.

And then—it happened so quickly that Jesus, although his gaze was fixed on Nathanael's back, did not see it at all—and then, Nathanael moved toward the approaching milites, his arms held straight up over his head: In a posture of surrender? In a gesture of conciliation? In a stance of strength? Perhaps he shouted. Jesus wasn't sure. It was all over so quickly, so incredibly. The straightened fingers of the hands flinched and stiffened into writhing claws. The elbows folded and the arms drooped—lower, lower, lower. His chin pressed toward his chest as he seemed to look down and examine the ground, or his feet, or...his stomach. His body wavered and slumped. He dropped to his knees, his hands now out of sight, probably pressing against a wound, futilely attempting to stem the warm, slippery flow of his life blood.

Jesus could see beyond Nathanael now: the soldier who had jammed his sword into the unarmed man's gut, his sword half extended in a position to strike again; the other milites each poised in readiness for battle; in the distance beyond them, beyond the fluttering flames of the torches, the ominous, moonlit walls of the Temple Mount.

Nathanael fell to his side, his forearms and hands pressed against his stomach, his knees bent and pulled up in a defensive position that had come much too late.

James, still standing in front of the Optio, let his arm fall to his side, the handle of the ridiculous sword now loose in his hand.

John pulled his knife away from the Optio's throat and, on his knees, stared at his fallen friend.

Simon, his head raised so that he had been able to watch what was happening, released his hold on the Optio and allowed himself to be rolled off as the Roman leader struggled to his feet.

Jesus pulled himself from Andrew's grasp and ran to Nathanael's side, dropping to his knees and pushing his fingers beneath Nathanael's hands, pushing against the throbbing, sticky warmth of the wound. The pulsing ooze collected beneath the pressure of his palm, slipped between his fingers, spread in hot rivulets across the back of his hand.

He was only distantly aware of Simon's desperate plea from behind him. "Heal him, Teacher."

"Teacher!" Andrew's hoarse cry scuttled into the darkness.

A steady, unremitting moan, as though from the mountain itself, rose and fell, rose and fell, rose and fell. It was John.

"Oh, my God," James droned. "Oh, my God. Oh, my God."

Across an endless tapestry that was Jesus' memory, a line of human beings, woven in pain and suffering, stretched from horizon to horizon. In the midst of this line of misery, the Son of Man moved, hand outstretched, touching, soothing, restoring—healing—one person, another person, still another: the blind, the crippled, the deaf, the deformed, the deranged, the paralyzed, the leprous, the unloved. The high-pitched, undulating wails of the untouched, of the unhealed, reverberated across the desolation of the tapestry. The Son of Man moved on. Behind him, as well as ahead of him, humanity writhed in awful, unremitting anguish.

"Nathanael!" Jesus sobbed, his forehead pressed against Nathanael's ear. "I'm here. I won't let you die!" Even as he spoke the promise, he knew that it was one he couldn't keep. Out of the corner of his eye, he could see that the blood was collecting on the ground now in a black pool. His hand—his useless, powerless hand—glistened red in the strange light of the torches.

Nathanael shuddered. His lips moved, forming deliberate, silent words that Jesus strained to hear. "...forever." The final word was "forever".

"Forever!" Jesus repeated. His throat constricted painfully, preventing him from saying more. He felt Nathanael tense, the muscles seeming to give one final earthly squeeze. And then...and then, Jesus felt the body let go. The lungs stopped gasping for breath, the heart stopped its frantic beat, the bloody hands atop Jesus' hands ceased pressing against the awful wound.

Silence! The night felt empty, impersonal. Death blanketed Jesus' soul with its suffocating indifference. Still on his knees, he straightened up and stared blankly at the fluttering flame of a torch.

"It was an accident." The soldier's words hung lifeless in the night air.

Jesus let his attention drift to the sword, still red with Nathanael's blood. He studied its shape, estimated its length, allowed himself to wonder about its heft. He raised his head to look up into the eyes of the young man, eyes that spoke of bewilderment and fear.

The eyes flicked briefly to the Optio and then back to Nathanael's shell. "I'm sorry," the young man said.

"Forget the dead man!" The angry voice came from behind Jesus. "People die every day." The Optio was at Jesus' side now, looming over the body. "It's our job to kill people," he added, almost to himself.

Jesus slowly stood up, his gaze locked with that of the remorseful milite. What was there to say? The Optio was correct. The young man was a soldier. It was the job of a soldier to kill people. The tragedy here… Oh, God! The tragedy was not the body that lay bloody and lifeless at his feet? How was that possible? The image of Nathanael shrugging his shoulders and striding ahead of him flashed through Jesus' memory. Nathanael had known God! Nathanael had known the kingdom of heaven. Nathanael had found Forever. There was nothing tragic about Nathanael. This young milite, this soldier who was not a soldier, his soul bloody and torpid, was the tragedy.

The Optio was issuing orders now; soldiers were moving in response. To Jesus, it was as though a door of time had been opened and immediately slammed shut. In that flashing glimpse of somewhere else, everything he thought he knew had been challenged and affirmed. Now—reluctantly acknowledging Now—he existed in a place of incomprehensible loss. Unemotionally he scanned the blank faces of Andrew, of James and John, of Simon. Dispassionately he held out his hands and watched as his wrists were bound with rope. Passively, in the midst of the milites, he strode at military pace toward the Kidron Bridge that arched over the valley toward the East Gate of the Temple Mount.

24

From the deep shade beneath the canopy of the fig tree, Jesus watches. Outside the somber walls of the city, three wooden crosses lean at odd angles, three lifeless trees on a barren hill that drops westward into the Valley of Hinnom, the abhorred place. Three distorted shapes, once human beings, hang splayed in triumphant decay.

Overhead, twisting and reaching, scarred by an eternity of injuries, muscular gray branches spread toward infinity. The musty odor of earth hangs heavily beneath the large, deeply lobed leaves—the aroma of decay, of fecundity, of birth. Life is the tree's silent, eternal intent, its cosmic promise.

A fig, cracking in ripeness, falls. Jesus gazes at it tranquilly, assimilating its purple toughness, anticipating the oozing white pulp that is the fig's ripeness. It is the end. It is the beginning. He breathes deeply, passionately, of the fertile loam on which he rests. For the first time he experiences again the white inner rind, the seed mass bound with blood-like flesh—the womb of everlasting life.

Printed in the United States
62284LVS00005B/151-249

9 781424 155699